Strange Brew...

"I'm far too warm," I said. "Please, Mrs. Venefica, perhaps the tea wasn't a good idea."

"No, it's a beautiful idea!" she crowed, and reached for the kettle. I could see the steam rising through the vents in the top of the pot. She had obviously loaded it with tea leaves. I thought of Ben Magruder and the list of exotic drugs that had been found in the garroted girl's stomach. I began to shake in my chair.

"A little mixture of my own," she told me as she lifted the pot and poured a cup of tea for me. Our eyes met. She smiled. "Drink it down, Aimee," she said, and began to giggle.

I was frightened, very frightened. I could hear Ben Magruder's warning voice once again: "Get out of there, Aimee, or fear for your life!"

I lifted the teacup to my lips and the scent went into my nose. It was like no other tea I had ever smelled!

The Diabolist

MARY ANNE DREW

AVON
PUBLISHERS OF BARD, CAMELOT, DISCUS, EQUINOX AND FLARE BOOKS

THE DIABOLIST is an original publication of Avon Books.
This work has never before appeared in any form.

AVON BOOKS
A division of
The Hearst Corporation
959 Eighth Avenue
New York, New York 10019

Copyright © 1975 by Bruce Cassiday.
Published by arrangement with the author.

ISBN: 0-380-00235-3

All rights reserved, which includes the right
to reproduce this book or portions thereof in
any form whatsoever. For information address
Lenniger Literary Agency, 437 Fifth Avenue,
New York, New York 10016.

First Avon Printing, February, 1975.

AVON TRADEMARK REG. U.S. PAT. OFF. AND
FOREIGN COUNTRIES, REGISTERED TRADEMARK—
MARCA REGISTRADA, HECHO EN CHICAGO, U.S.A.

Printed in the U.S.A.

PART ONE:

Lora Blake

Chapter One

Don and I were married on June 23rd, and moved into a studio apartment in Greenwich Village. After three months we bought a house in Coldwater, Connecticut, so that Don could be within commuting distance of New York, where he worked for IBM.

For a month after we moved into the house I looked for a job, and found one in October with a local residence hall for career girls. I had done some social work in New York between college and marriage, and I was hired as Assistant Director of the Fairfield Residence Hall.

It was there that the strange happenings I am about to relate really began.

I remember clearly when it started—the first day on the job. Don drove me to the front of the building on Summer Street on his way to the railroad station.

"Good luck, Aimee," he said, kissing me on the cheek.

"Take care," I said, waving to him and running up the steps. I never did believe in watching him drive off like some insecure, middle-class housewife.

From the very first, I liked the brick building that housed the Fairfield Residence Hall, and knew that it would be a fine place to work. I felt that I had been lucky in love, lucky in marriage, and now would be lucky in work.

The building had wide steps leading up to a double door in carved paneling. Eight two-story columns upheld a porch roof, fronted by a classic pediment and topped by a widow's walk of fluted supports. The building was four stories high, with a clean, red brick front, broken up by double-hung windows, all bordered by white shutters.

The blending of neo-classic and Colonial created a structure at once graceful and clear-lined. The area between the sidewalk and the brick wall was planted with lawn and rhododendrons alternating with smaller shrubs. The lawn was protected by an iron fence, each post of which was topped by a speared cast iron arrowhead.

It was all very New Englandy and very small-townish. And that suited me fine. I had come from a very small town myself, far off in upper Massachusetts.

I stepped inside the main corridor and turned to the right where Mrs. Grant's office was located. Mrs. Grant was waiting for me at her door with a bright smile. Of an indeterminate age—possibly in her fifties—she wore severe clothes which went well with her lithe frame. She had touched-up her brown hair with a blonde rinse, and she tended to move with the kind of alacrity normally associated with pep pills. An intense, intelligent, determined woman she was.

I liked her.

"Good morning, Aimee," she said, that bright smile flickering on and off. "You're right on time!"

"My husband has a thing about punctuality," I responded. "An IBM trait, I'm told."

"Put your coat in the hall closet," Mrs. Grant suggested. "Then we'll take a tour of the building. You haven't met all the staff yet."

"Yes, ma'am," I murmured, and hung my coat in the closet next to all the others. Was Mrs. Grant trying to impress me that she was all director? Or was she trying to impress herself?

To tell the truth, it did not take as long as I had suspected it might. I met the Refectory Director, a mousy type named Miss Ross; the Recreational Director, Miss Tansy, a bouncy woman who would have passed for a physical education teacher in a high school; the Personnel Director; the Social Director; and the Resident Director.

Then I met the two Floor Directors. The top floors of the building were given over to small cubicles in which the girls lived, with the bottom floors taken up with administrative offices, the kitchen and dining room, and the recreation room.

In charge of the Fourth Floor was Mrs. Venefica, a rather ancient but apparently sincere woman who was thin, trembling, wiry, sinewy, and waspish, all at once. She had eyes as bright as a crow's, and a face that was far less lined than you would think it should be for her advanced age. I assumed she must have been in her sixties. And yet she was alert—painfully alert—and almost aggressive in her insistance on the social amenities.

She had an office at the head of the stairs with the window overlooking Summer Street and Wagner's Department Store across the street. She kept a number of potted plants on the window sill, and a dozen more shrubs growing in larger planters placed about the office.

Mrs. Grant stood first on one foot and then on the other as Mrs. Venefica greeted me. She shook hands with me, as I have described, as if she wanted to make sure we were empathizing with each other. She seemed to be studying me carefully, and I assumed that she was simply very interested in human beings and was exercising her outgoing nature to its utmost.

"I understand that you went to Wellesley College," she said in her high, rather tremulous voice, as she continued to hold my hand, gripping it tightly.

"Yes, ma'am," I said, withdrawing from her grasp with an obvious effort.

"It's always nice to meet new people," she sighed, as if she did not always get the chance to do so. "I do hope you'll be at home with our lovely group of girls!"

"I'm sure I shall be," I said politely.

"We have a very select clientele," she observed. "Clean, attractive young women."

"Do they all work in Coldwater?" I asked, as if to fill in the moments until I could get away.

"Some do, some don't," said Mrs. Venefica. "But they're all wonderful people."

"There are twelve of them on this floor," said Mrs. Grant, turning to me. "One of your jobs, Aimee, will be to entice more girls to move into the top floor here. At the present time, this floor is operating at a loss." She seemed to direct this barb at Mrs. Venefica. I wondered briefly why she did not get rid of Mrs. Venefica if she seemed to be driving the residents away—as Mrs. Grant seemed to be implying.

The older woman could not have been less disturbed. "They come and they go," she beamed. I could tell by the tremor in her voice that she was very old, although the firmness of her flesh belied her advanced age. She turned to me, and I could almost feel the bright, piercing quality of her glance.

"You're a very pretty young woman, Mrs. Hammond."

I flushed. "Thank you. I—I do hope we shall get along well."

"We shall," promised Mrs. Venefica, again reaching out and taking my hand in hers. "We shall."

Mrs. Grant elbowed me aside. "We've got to get her to work," she said quickly, insinuating herself between Mrs. Venefica and me. "Come, Aimee."

"It's been nice meeting you, Aimee," said Mrs. Venefica, and as she smiled I noticed that she winced momentarily and her hand flew involuntarily to her side under her left breast.

We went out into the hallway, leaving Mrs. Venefica staring after us.

"Old frump," murmured Mrs. Grant as she guided me down the stairs to the third floor. "She fancies herself housemother to all the residents. She herds them around like her own special children. And when someone who is a little different from those already there moves in we never seem able to retain her."

"I don't quite understand what you're saying."

Mrs. Grant snorted and shook her head. "Please

don't mind me, Aimee. I'm indulging in recriminations, I'm afraid. It's just that—" She hesitated. "Well, if a new fourth floor resident doesn't fit in with Mrs. Venefica's ideas about community living, then she is made unwelcome and leaves."

"Mrs. Venefica makes herself unwelcome?"

"No. I mean, her girls—" Mrs. Grant laughed, that quick, glinting flash of teeth and abrupt burst of amusement, and then the blank façade again. "See? I call them 'hers'. Of course, they're ours, aren't they? Yet if one comes in and doesn't fit in—out she goes."

"But who decides this?"

Mrs. Grant shook her head. "I don't want to talk about it, Aimee. Here we are on the second floor. You see the fine setup for recreation?"

And the rest was routine.

I settled into the job with no trouble at all. Don left me off each morning, and picked me up at the close of the day. We furnished our little house on the outskirts of Coldwater, and within ten days I was completely broken in to the job.

That was the day Mrs. Venefica—

It happened this way:

I had just completed the rundown on the November-December calendar and had carried it up to Jill Towers on the second floor for typing and mimeographing which I saw Mrs. Venefica standing at the top of the stairs looking down at me. I do not know why, but there was something completely compelling about her presence at that moment: the look in her eyes, the particular stance of her thin body, the vibrations in the air between us. Oh, I know it was simply imagination, but I did get a start.

She saw I was disturbed.

"Oh, Aimee," she called down to me. "Do come up and have a cup of tea with me! Won't you, please? It's been so long since we chatted."

I glanced about me, perhaps subconsciously seeking escape. Mrs. Venefica simply was not my idea of an ideal companion. Not that there was anything about

11

her that I could actually put my finger on. But somehow her presence was unsettling.

I thought of that small office and the plants growing in the window sill and I will admit I was not at all happy at the thought of spending fifteen minutes chatting with her.

But I was a new employee, and I was trying to make myself agreeable to everyone at the establishment, and I took the coward's way out.

"Thank you very much," I said, and began to mount the stairs toward her.

She nodded and I followed her as she retreated to her office around the corner.

It was like a hothouse in there. The sun was bright outside, and it was a little warm for October. But she had the heat up on the radiator until I could almost feel the moisture touching the surface of my skin.

Mrs. Venefica minced toward her desk and sat down behind it. I could see that she had a tray out, with two tea cups and a pot of tea all ready for me. Two spoons, sugar, and a bit of mint leaf lay on the side of each saucer.

"It's very nice of you, Mrs. Venefica," I began.

"Think nothing of it, child," she said with a toothy little smile. She had even white teeth, obviously not her own. I wondered again how old she must be. Yet there was nothing old about those bright perceptive eyes. They were watching me carefully as I sipped at the tea and tried to appear pleased at her attentions.

The tea had a odd taste, but I am no gourmet when it comes to beverages, and I assumed that it was some exotic brand that I should be very much up on and that I should be very pleased at the privilege of tasting.

"It's delightful," I said finally.

Her brow rose.

"The tea!" I said.

"Oh, of course," she responded. "Try some nice mint leaf."

I nodded, picking up a piece of mint leaf and floating it in the tea.

"Do you grow your own mint?"

She smiled. "Oh, yes. I grow a great number of interesting things." She turned her small bird-like body in the chair and beamed at her window garden. Then she was staring at me again. "Do you like your new job?"

I nodded. What business was that of hers? I wondered. "Yes, thank you. Very much."

"I'm glad."

I sipped my tea, wishing Mrs. Grant would summon me on the intercom.

She did not.

I finished the tea finally, making small talk with Mrs. Venefica, which proved to be quite unproductive and time-wasting, and then rose to leave.

Mrs. Venefica accompanied me to the door. "It's very nice of you to come—" she began, and then at that moment I saw all the color leave her face. It was as if she had collapsed inwardly, as if everything that was holding her together had gone out of her. She began to slump against me, and I turned quickly to try to lead her to her desk chair.

But she was extremely strong for her size. She clawed at me, trying to keep herself from falling to the floor, and I did the best I could to carry her to the chair in which I had been sitting. At one moment our eyes met, and I was shocked to see that her eyes were absolutely empty—that is, I seemed to be looking into some kind of bottomless pit as I stared into them. There was no sense of color in the pupils at all, not black, not any color in the spectrum. Perhaps they seemed red—no. I cannot say that. I do not really know *what* color they were.

At the same moment, I felt myself spin through space, into another planet complex somewhere, or perhaps into a totally foreign galaxy. I was conscious of space and time and brilliant light and a great deal of searing heat. I know I am expressing this badly, but it was simply an impression that was momentary, and endless, all at once. There was a buzzing in my ears, a buzzing that quickly came and went.

I seemed whirled about endlessly in time—but of course it was only an instantaneous feeling—burning in that heat, with a world of redness and white light about me. I had no orientation, that is, I was at no one place in space. I was everywhere, and I was nowhere.

Very strange.

It was only a momentary vision.

Then I was back in Mrs. Venefica's office, and she was slumped in the chair I had just vacated, and Mrs. Grant was chaffing Mrs. Venefica's hands and talking to her, and Mrs. Venefica's eyes were beginning to open.

"Dear me, dear me," murmured Mrs. Venefica. I shrank back against the wall, suddenly more tired than I had ever been in my life before.

But no one was paying me the slightest attention. Mrs. Grant was working over Mrs. Venefica, and then Mrs. Hope, the Floor Director from number two came up to help, and soon Mrs. Venefica was back at her desk as if nothing had happened.

Dazed, I walked downstairs with Mrs. Grant.

"She gets these spells," she told me. "Sorry you had to be there. It's unnerving." She sighed. "I suppose the dear old soul will leave us some day."

Die?

"We don't even know how old she is," murmured Mrs. Grant, with that quick, brilliant smile, and then blankness. "You look pale, Aimee," she observed, suddenly.

"I'm—I'm all right," I whispered.

She watched me as I went back to my office adjoining hers. I *was* all right. Just a little dizziness, just a little at loose ends. In fifteen minutes I had forgotten all about Mrs. Venefica's "attack" and was working at top speed on the next week's menu.

The dream occurred in the middle of the night. I was alone in a vast world of treeless and grassless wasteland—a scorched earth, a moonscape that was not the moon. It was burning hot everywhere. I could not see flames anywhere, but I could sense sulphuric ragings from hollows and fissures that pocked the landscape. The sky was purple, great clouds of swirling intensity gouting up—a vaporous exhalation from some nether blast furnace. Alone, alone, alone. I could not speak, for I had no mouth, I could not see, for I had no eyes, yet I could *sense* what I have already described.

Alone.

Then I was whirled through space as if by a rocket, or a force greater than all the rockets in existence. And I came back to my bed and lay there staring into Don's eyes.

The light by the bed was on. The clock said 2 a.m.

Don lay on his side, staring at me in great shock—shock that was on the borderline of horror.

"Aimee! Wake up!"

"I—I am awake, Don. What is it?" I was slightly dizzy, still, but trying to reorient myself.

It was the look in his eyes that brought me to full consciousness. He was frozen almost rigid, his mouth slightly open, his hands gripping my shoulders as if they would not let go.

And then I noticed something that almost set me weeping. I was lying there naked in bed—without a stitch of clothing on! I *always* wear pajamas to bed—and yet, now I had nothing on. And Don—Don knew that.

I cried out in embarrassment and turned quickly away from him. Pulling the bedclothes over me, I huddled there in an agony of shame. I knew I was blushing, I could feel my cheeks grow hot.

"Don't look, Don!" I whispered. "Please! You know I *try* to be modern—but I'm just an old-fashioned girl. I'm not used—used to this!"

"I'm not looking, Aimee," he said calmly, in a muffled tone, and I knew he was not.

I climbed out of bed and ran to the chest of drawers. But as I stepped across the room my bare feet became entangled in the bottoms of my pajamas. I leaned down quickly and stepped into them, then found the tops on the bed. I slipped into them quickly and climbed back under the covers.

I was shaking all over—from chagrin, from the reaction to my embarrassment, and from real fear. What had happened? I could not remember *anything*.

"Don," I said, turning to him. "Please. Look at me."

Before he turned over to face me I saw something that absolutely horrified me. Don's pajama tops were torn at the shoulder. I could see streaks of still-bleeding scratches along his shoulder blade.

He faced me, his eyes wary. "I'm sorry, Aimee. I had to wake you up. I knew—I knew you had no idea what you were doing."

"Doing?" I shook my head dazedly. "I was dreaming. Did I scream?" I smiled feebly.

"Not at all," he said flatly. "You—you—" I was astonished to see the slightest hint of a blush on his cheeks. Then his face stiffened. "You're sure you don't remember a thing?"

"Not a thing," I said.

It must have been the sincerity of my expression that convinced him, for he suddenly relaxed and lay there apparently trying to compose himself.

"What did I do?" I asked again.

He looked at the ceiling, frowning. "Aimee," he said. "I can't really describe it all, because I know how you feel about—about all that sort of thing."

I could feel a sudden beating of my heart as it slammed against my ribs. He was delicately skirting the subject because of my feelings. And there was only one subject he knew bothered me: explicit sex talk. I *knew* with an intuitive flash that I must have done something—in my sleep, in my dream—that startled him and embarrassed him. If it was strange enough, and wild enough, to startle *him,* what might it do to me if I knew?

I leaned over and touched his chin. "Don. Did I—did I do something—?" Then I realized that I had awakened without my pajamas on. "My clothes?"

"That," said Don, "and more!" His face relaxed in sudden remembrance. "Honey, you were—were like a tiger!"

Then I understood. To my everlasting shame and

mortification, I understood. "That scratch on your shoulder?"

"You did it!" said Don, smiling abruptly.

I flushed deeply. "You're not telling me the truth!"

"It was—it was as if something possessed you, darling!" he said, propping himself up on one elbow and reaching out to caress my hair. "If you don't remember, I'm not about to tell you!"

"Did I mean to—to harm you?"

He threw back his head and laughed loudly. "Far from it!" he said, as soon as he could control himself. "It was strictly—" he groped for the right word—"love?"

I turned away from him, unable to speak. Tears crept into my eyes. I had been brought up to be a completely modest woman. And now here my husband was telling me that I had turned into a wanton in the middle of the night—during a dream!

The scratch. The pajamas. He could not be lying. I had—

What had I done? What had happened to me?

"Darling," he said soothingly, reaching out to me and turning me toward him. "Don't worry about it. It was—it was an unforgettable—"

He kissed me and I could feel the warmth of his love envelope me. And that was all that really mattered.

Don let me off at the front of the Residence Hall at seven-thirty and I hurried inside. Mrs. Grant was in her office, drinking coffee from a steaming cardboard carton.

"Aimee!" she cried out. "You'll have to take over the fourth floor today. Mrs. Venefica had some kind of attack last night. Whatever it was, she was found in the hallway by Lenore Ulrich. Lenore got her to bed and called the doctor. She's all right, I guess."

"Oh?" I said casually.

"She's had these attacks before, of course. I'm afraid she must be ailing. But, really—" snapped Mrs. Grant with that quick smile, that quick grimace—"to throw a fit at two a.m. in the morning!"

Chapter Two

One of the reasons Don and I moved to Coldwater was the presence there of Ben Magruder. It was, in fact, Ben who had told us that the little cottage we bought was for sale. I had met Ben on my first job in Spanish Harlem in New York, where I was doing social work.

Ben Magruder was much older than Don and I. He often said that there was not a generation gap between him and me—but *two*. He wore a full beard, had red hair and green eyes, and liked to loll around the tiny cottage he had bought in the Ridges in sandals and open T shirt, with his tortoise-shelled glasses pushed up into his flaming, red hair.

"They called us Bohemians when I lived as a youth in Greenwich Village," Ben told me once. "Now there are no more Bohemians, but there are 'hippies' and 'freakouts.' Perhaps I'm a freakout."

He had a booming laugh, and he laughed fairly often. The world and its foibles amused him. Don and I amused him, for some odd reason, and both of us liked him. I suppose it all had to do with me. I do not mean at all that Ben Magruder was sexually attracted to me—but he was interested in my past.

I remember the first time I met him in Harlem. We were both in a tiny drugstore on a corner of a dilapidated section where only Spanish was spoken—and then with a particularly harsh Puerto Rican accent. We were both looking for a tin of aspirin: I for a headache, and he for another reason. He said later that he used aspirin as a conversation opener to get to the more important items on the store's shelves.

Actually, he thought I was the clerk in the store, and I thought he was the proprietor. After blundering along in bad Spanish for some moments with each other, we both discovered we were not getting anywhere, spoke in English simultaneously, and burst out laughing. After which, we left the tiny store without buying anything and began regaling each other with our impressions of the neighborhood, watched attentively and with scorn by most of the Puerto Rican children. *"Gringos,"* they seemed to be saying of us. "Crazy *gringos*."

My job was routine, but Ben Magruder's was not. He was researching a book on Caribbean voodoo, and he was using the background of Espan-Harlem to prove how hard old superstitions die. He told me that he had discovered literally dozens of stores in Espan-Harlem where you could buy voodoo charms, voodoo incantations, and voodoo recipes for curses, for good luck, and for *el amor*.

He was a fascinating man. And it probably would have become simply a one-time meeting had I not accidentally mentioned during a pause in the voluble conversation that I had a witch's name.

I remember to this moment how he has stared at me, his green eyes very still, his body very stiff.

"A witch's name?"

"Well, a possessed girl's name, anyway." I laughed.

"Say it!"

"Parris," I said lightly. I had the idea that he would not know what I was talking about.

"Elizabeth Parris," he murmured half under his breath. "Abigail Williams. Mercy Lewis."

I suppose my mouth dropped open in a nonsensical gape. "Yes! How did you know?"

He shook his head as if unable to comprehend the density of the female mind. "I *said* I was researching witchcraft and voodoo. Do you think I would not know the details of America's greatest witch hunt?"

"And the voodoo woman? The witch? Tituba, wasn't it?" he mused. Then those green eyes narrowed as he studied me again. "What was your father's name, my dear?"

I felt myself flushing. I had brought up the subject because it was an amusing one to me, since I had absolutely no use for witches, witches' curses, or devils, now that it was all so far away in my past. But I knew I had made a mistake mentioning it to Ben Magruder. He *believed*. I could tell he did. And I did *not* believe. So much for opposites.

"Actually, his name was William Parris." I said no more.

"William." Ben Magruder closed his eyes. "I wonder—"

"Wonder what?"

"If you could be related to Reverend Samuel Parris," Ben Magruder mused in a low voice.

"But don't you see, I am not only related to Reverend Samuel, I *am* a Samuel Parris."

He reached out and gripped my wrist. "You mean—"

"I was born and raised in Salem," I told him weakly.

He relaxed. He let go of my wrist, turned from me, staring far off into the distance at the cluttered street, and slowly rubbed his forefinger across his beard.

"Interesting," he murmured. "Interesting."

And that was the last time he mentioned my background, but it was not the last time I saw him. We had dinner one night with Don, whom I was dating, and when we were married, Ben invited us up to spend a weekend in his house in Coldwater.

And, I say, it was he who told us of the availability of the cottage on Cold Brook Drive, which we later bought.

So, naturally, we had him over for dinner several nights after I had begun work at Fairfield Residence Hall.

Ben Magruder was the same as ever, but when he came into our small living room and stood under the bright light, I was suddenly shocked at his appearance. Why, he was an old man! I had never felt that way about him before. Actually, he did not look well. I wondered if he was having trouble with his health.

It would never do to ask.

Don and Ben were laughing together and Don was pouring drinks for all of us, as I went out into the kitchen to see to the dinner. It was one of my first dinners cooked in Coldwater, and the very first for a guest in our own home. I am not a fussy housewife, but because Ben was our best friend, I wanted this meal to be perfect.

And it was while I stood over the pots on the stove, that I suddenly thought of Mrs. Venefica and her close litle office at the top of the Hall. It seemed for the moment that I was inside that very room once again, stifling in the unmoving, stale air. I could hardly breathe. I moved quickly back from the boiling pots, thinking of those strange plants of Mrs. Venefica's, and then I do not know what I did.

The next thing I knew I was standing in the living room, and the air was clean and my head began to clear. But both Don and Ben were staring up at me from their chairs, holding their glasses in their hands and not saying anything.

I put my wrist to my forehead and blinked once or twice.

Don was up, immediately solicitous. "What's wrong, Aimee?"

"My head," I said softly. "I just felt—*dizzy*—for a moment." I laughed. "It's nothing." Indeed, it was nothing. I felt all right now and I despised myself for having had that momentary lapse. Excitement. Anxiety. Nerves.

Ben Magruder sipped at his drink, his sharp green eyes still on mine. "You're acting quite like a married woman, Aimee," he said, with an obvious inflection on "married."

I shook my head with a light laugh. "Oh, I'm not that way—Ben! Please!"

"I apologize for suggesting such an—*unnatural*—thing as pregnancy," Ben said languidly, and Don burst into laughter. "But, seriously, Aimee—*are* you all right?"

"Yes," I said airily. I was blushing at Ben's mention of pregnancy. Don calls me a prude. Perhaps.

Don grinned. He said casually to Ben, "It's the dreams, really."

Ben's eyes were locked on my face again. "Dreams?"

I stared at Don. At his insistence, I had told him about that strange recurring dream of burning, for it had come again three times after the first night. And although nothing else had happened but the dream in those succeeding times, it was beginning to unnerve me. Every time I dropped off to sleep I half expected to wake up in that deserted landscape, burning, burning, burning . . .

"She dreams she's on fire, Ben," said Don, taking his drink and finishing it off. He picked up Ben's empty glass and carried them both out into the kitchen for more. I stood in the middle of the living room, arrested in my route back to the dinner, facing Ben Magruder's probing eyes.

"Burning, Aimee?"

I nodded. "Yes."

"Like a *witch*?" His voice faltered.

"No!" I cried, annoyed at his quick insight. "It's just a dream! Nothing else!"

"You're becoming strident, my dear," he said with that gentle smile.

And indeed I was. But for the life of me I could not take an unemotional attitude about that recurring dream. Whenever I was reminded of it I began trembling and breathing hard. I am a singularly unemotional, very unperturable young woman. Anything unusual is decidedly unexpected in my life.

"Tell me," he said.

I did. In straightforward, uncluttered phrases, I told him as best I could. The deserted landscape. The heat. And then the sensation of being whirled through space.

He listened, nodding now and then, but said nothing when I had finished. In fact, Don came back in the room at that moment, and I went and got the dinner ready.

When I returned with the food, they were discussing pro football, and I could not have cared less about *that*.

After we were through dinner we sat around for a long time on the enclosed back porch and watched the fireflies light up the night. Then finally Ben Magruder leaned back in his chair, his eyes half closed and asked:

"How do you like your job, Aimee?"

"Oh, I love it!" I said. "After the trials and tribulations of social work in Harlem, this is the easiest job I've ever had!"

"It sounds like the best thing in the world for you."

"Oh, I think it is, Ben! I like the girls and—" I hesitated, because I could suddenly think of nothing more to say.

"And what?" Ben prompted.

"And all the rest of the women," I went on. "It's an interesting place. Rather old-fashioned. But very nice."

Ben frowned. "You haven't said anything about the *people* who work there," he told me.

"No," I said. "Because you're going to meet them first hand. I just learned that today. We're having our regular October Social on Saturday night. You're free to come, aren't you, Ben?"

He grinned. "I wouldn't miss it for the world."

The October Social was held in the large dining room of the Residence Hall. All the girls were on their best behavior. By the time the party was held, I knew them by name, and was by then completely compatible with the rest of the staff.

Only Mrs. Venefica was her own enigmatic self, tottering about all around the dining room as she did on her beloved fourth floor. She had a way of peering at everyone nearsightedly and smiling broadly, as if amused at something no one else could discern. It was a bit disconcerting, but when you looked at Mrs. Venefica closely, you realized that she was very old and possibly not all there in the head.

Of course, I knew that she was very much all there

in the head. But there was no need to make strangers wonder any more than they ordinarily did.

Mrs. Grant was the total hostess, and went about the group meeting everyone and welcoming them to the party, smiling her bright, quick smile, and then turning away and rushing about somewhere else.

Mrs. Venefica's fourth floor girls all sat with her when it came time to eat, and they began singing odd little songs before the food was served. I had not yet been able to get through to the girls in Mrs. Venefica's clan to try to find out what they were up to, but there was nothing that could be done now, and no one seemed to notice. When the food came, the girls lapsed into silence and let Mrs. Venefica carry the conversation for them.

The rest of the residents at the Hall seemed to be enjoying themselves and conversed openly with the many guests, including of course Ben Magruder, and the husbands of all the women workers on the staff. Mr. Grant, I learned, had died some years ago. I actually had never been told that until the night of the party.

Ben Magruder seemed to be enjoying himself. I caught sight of him once while I was rushing about helping serve a drink, and I saw him wandering around with his hands clasped behind his back, staring at paintings that had been on the walls of the hall for years and years. Then he began examining some of the indoor plants that stood about in pots. He talked to one or two of the girls who lived at the Hall and went to college at the Coldwater branch of the state university, and then he was off somewhere else.

At one point, I turned around from a knot of chattering girls to see him standing in the entryway to the Hall, staring out through the glass panes of the front door. I then observed him moving through the doors and bending over as if to pick up something on the front porch.

Dear old Ben! I thought. He was such a cuddly old bear of a man!

After the dinner, we cleared the floor for dancing, and there were several couples who danced—some in the old-fashioned manner, and others in the new. But it was simply not a very exciting dance.

There were movies after that, and then tea and cakes, later in the evening. People began drifting out soon after ten. I helped in the kitchen while a group of girls cleared the tables and brought in the dishes to be washed.

Don drove Ben Magruder home and came back to pick me up at midnight.

We drove most of the way home in silence. I lay with my head back against the seat and my eyes closed.

"Ben's worried," said Don finally.

"About what?" I asked drowsily.

"About you."

"What on earth for?"

"The dreams, I guess," said Don.

"I haven't had the dream for days now!"

"I told him that. He's still worried."

"But whatever for?"

"The Hall, I guess," said Don uneasily.

I sat up, staring ahead of me at the winding, darkened roadway. "The Hall? I think Ben's gone soft in the head!" I snorted.

Don sighed. "So do I, actually." He shook his head. "Anyway, I think he'll be calling you about it."

"About what?" I asked with annoyance.

"He'll tell you."

And tell me he did.

He did not telephone. He drove up to the house in his ancient Alfa Romeo.

It was the night Don was in New York taking his lecture class in sales principles. And I was all alone trying to watch television without falling asleep.

After the Alfa Romeo had stopped in the driveway I could hear Ben's heavy footsteps on the steps. Then the doorbell rang.

"Hi, Ben!" I was really glad to see him. When Don is away from home I get bored being alone.

He came in, smiling at me and shrugging out of his sports jacket. He was a burly man anyway, and the

25

woolen jackets he wore made him look three times as big as he already was.

We had coffee.

Then he started.

"You've got to quit work at the Hall," he said in a no-nonsense voice.

"I will *not*!" I came right back challengingly. Somehow, I had guessed at the purpose of his visit.

"You have to, Aimee. It's—it's dangerous."

"Dangerous?"

"Yes! Dangerous! To your health. To your life, even." He looked away, seemingly embarrassed at what he was saying.

I did not blame him for being embarrassed. "That's ridiculous, Ben!"

He shook his head stubbornly. "No. It is *not* ridiculous. There is something—something about that place—" His voice dropped.

"This is absurd! I invited you to a party! You came to the Hall! And the next thing I know, you're telling me I have to quit my job there!"

"From the moment I got into that place I could feel something was not quite right," Ben said steadily, sipping at his coffee. "Believe me, Aimee, when I say that I am experienced in things of the occult. I could *feel* the evil quality of the air! Someone—someone there—is capable of—casting an evil spell!"

I sat up straight. "Oh, you've been writing another one of those books of yours," I snapped. "You eat and sleep witchcraft!"

"But there *is* necromancy there, Aimee! I don't want you mixed up in it!"

I stared at him in astonishment. "That's nonsense, Ben."

"No," whispered Ben. His eyes came up to my face. I could feel him leaning closer to me. Uncomfortably, I began squirming in the chair. "I took the opportunity of looking around the Hall," he told me evenly. "There were potted plants that might bear investigation. And those Latin chants the girls sang before they ate—I wouldn't certify *them* as pure. But there's no question about the fact that there is a *witch's mark on the doorstep.*"

I gaped at him again in disbelief.

"I lifted the doormat because I had a feeling, Aimee." He leaned back, took more coffee, and then set the cup down. There was no sound in the room. "A pentacle had been drawn under the mat! The witch's sign."

Of course I had heard of a pentacle. It is a five-pointed star, with the lines connecting the points continuously throughout the symbol. When a man or woman wants to call up evil spirits, he stands in the center of the pentacle, where evil forces cannot touch him. At least, that is what those who believe in witchcraft say.

"As you know," Ben rumbled in that deep voice of his, "a person practicing witchcraft uses the pentacle to keep other witches from putting the spell on him. Someone at the Hall is practicing demonology, Aimee! It's a certain fact!"

In spite of myself, I shivered.

"And I suspect that *you're* the intended victim!"

"Oh, Ben!" I scoffed. "Do be a dear, and let's not talk about it! You know I will never believe in witchcraft!"

He stared at me sadly. "Perhaps you will someday, Aimee. Perhaps you'll *have to!*"

Poor Ben! He was considerably shaken when I saw him to the door to let him out. It only embarrassed me that he was so flustered because of concern for me.

As for me, I felt perfectly safe.

Chapter Three

If I remember correctly, it was two days after the October Social that Lora Blake came to live at Fairfield Residence Hall. A Monday, to be exact. There was nothing special about her arrival at the Hall, and any excitement she may have caused later was certainly not presaged by her very ordinary initial appearance.

She was seventeen or eighteen, I simply do not remember which, and she had just dropped out of her freshman year in college at the Coldwater branch of the University. I only saw her briefly on her first day at the Hall. Mousy hair, mousy face, mousy posture. She was a very forgettable person. Now that is not really nice, is it? Talking about a fellow human being that way?

Yet that was the way she struck me.

I gathered from a brief exchange of hellos that she was a rather reticent type; not reticent through vanity or any attempt to cover up superior attainments in mentality, but simply reticent through a kind of dull mediocrity. She was not bright, or outgoing, or in any way exceptional.

Mrs. Grant briefed me later in the day. She and I usually had a routine meeting every afternoon about three o'clock, during which we discussed the things to do the next day or the next week, and the things which needed immediate attention for the balance of the day. And at those meetings either of us could bring up any questions or discussions of procedure relating to the more touchy personal situations that always kept coming up at the Hall.

"Then there's Lora Blake," Mrs. Grant said, glancing up from her desk brightly at me, holding her forefinger on a typed sheet in front of her. "You've met her?"

"Yes," I said. "Very nice girl. Well brought up. Should be no problem." How little I knew about Lora Blake! But that was my first impression. And I was a well-trained social worker. So much for educational training and spot-character readings.

"Yes," said Mrs. Grant brightly. "She has no parents. Comes from a little town in Illinois. It seems her fiancé in Connecticut was killed in a motor accident."

"That's too bad," I heard myself saying, not really caring, of course, because Lora Blake had not made any definite impression on me.

"Yes. She's a shy little thing," Mrs. Grant went on. "I think we should put her in with the girls on the fourth floor."

"She's is a bit inner-oriented," I said, using the proper psychiatric jargon. "Yes. I believe she should have a strong peer group to identify with. I agree. The girls on the fourth floor have a camaraderie that might help."

"Good, good," mused Mrs. Grant, flashing that smile and reading a little more of the paper in front of her. "Apparently an uncle—her mother's brother—is the one who is paying for her residency here. It was he who enrolled her. And he lives in California."

"Well, let's hope there won't be any problems with her," I said cheerfully.

"I'm sure there won't be," Mrs. Grant said.

And we went on to something else.

I did not see Lora again for at least a week.

During that week I found a chance to take a quick look at the front porch of the Hall under the door mat. I had dismissed Ben Magruder's suspicions as the fanaticism of a man who was too wrapped up in the subjects about which he was writing to have a clear head. But I still wanted to check, to be sure that Ben was not making everything up.

No. The faint chalk outlines of a pentacle were visible on the concrete surface, all right—at least, it was a five-pointed star drawn with a kind of crudity that suggested either unfamiliarity with the symbol or an attempt to suggest unfamiliarity.

Hastily, I put the mat back in place and retired to my office to think about it.

It could be a joke. It could be the real thing. I had no way of discovering the truth. I did not want to believe Ben Magruder's claims without making sure he was basing his conclusions on actual facts.

But I had an idea that Ben's panic was a result more of his fears about my own strange recurring dream than it was a result of a clear logical conclusion based on the finding of the pentacle on the front porch. Also, I realized that he was hedging a bit about the "songs" the girls on the fourth floor had been singing at the party. So? They might have been singing incantations just for the fun of it. Mrs. Venefica was certainly a character, and her eccentricity actually made the girls rally around her more than they would around a more dull, average person. And the plants in the Hall? I remembered my own sense of being stifled by the closeness of Mrs. Venefica's office—but there was nothing specific that I could put my finger on. More speculation on Ben Magruder's part, of course.

And why would anyone want to put a spell on *me*?

It was too ridiculous.

Still—the pentacle existed.

I had no time to worry about pentacles and such nonsense, because Don's company chose that week to begin what they called a "severe reshuffling of personnel" after the appearance in *The Wall Street Journal* of a quarterly report that predicted disaster and ruin for business generally.

And so Don was away evenings, hustling about and looking important for the executives involved in cutting costs and effecting economies "without sacrificing efficiency or output in any way," as Don quoted them.

While the cool winds of economy were blowing, Don felt it necessary to stay late at the office. One night he had to stay overnight at a hotel in New York, and I did not see him for two days. It was not the happiest of times.

And it was at this point that I began to suspect that something was not quite right with Lora Blake.

She had been there ten days when she came to me in the office and asked me to help her.

I was startled. Usually, when someone asks me to help her, I accept the phrase as a polite way of requesting information, or simply as a manner of opening a serious discussion.

With Lora Blake, I could see at the outset, it was different with her. When she used the word "help," she meant it in a literal sense: the help you would give a drowning person, the help you would give a sick person, the help you would give someone trapped in a burning building.

"Help you?" I repeated, as I studied her. "In what way, Lora?"

She was twisting a handkerchief in her tiny hands. And her face was stricken with a kind of hopelessness. Her eyes were very blue, but very blank. And her face was a pasty white, with an almost unhealthy cast to it. We had given her all the physical tests required for residency at the Hall, and I knew she was not on drugs. Yet I wondered, once again, if she were an addict of some kind.

But a glance at her arms—she was wearing a sleeveless, knit top—showed there were no punctures in her skin.

"I don't know quite how to say it, Mrs. Hammond," she murmured. She looked up at me momentarily, but for some reason I seemed to frighten her, and she glanced immediately down, her blue eyes merely a flash.

"Try, Lora," I said kindly.

"It's just that—that I'm—I'm frightened—" She let the incomplete sentence hang there. I had the impression that she was frightened of some specific thing—but I could not really tell. And she did not seem to be able to put it into words.

31

I tried again. "Frightened of what, Lora?"

She glanced around the room—anywhere but into my eyes. And she kept on wringing that wretched handkerchief.

"I—I don't really know," she stammered, finally.

"But there must be something that frightens you," I said. "Try to tell me what it is."

"It's just—it's just—" And she stopped again, hanging her head hopelessly.

"Is it the girls?" I asked.

She looked up, her eyes startled. "Oh, no, of course not, Mrs. Hammond. They're all very nice! We—we have—we have a little kind of club up there." Her pale lips curved into a very small smile. I realized that she was a girl who seldom smiled. She seemed anxious.

"Then you like the club," I persisted.

"Oh yes. It's the first time I've ever really felt close to anyone my own age!" Lora said, burbling almost. "They're *very* nice!"

"Then what is the trouble?" I was beginning to sound irritated.

"I'm—I'm frightened," she said. "That's all."

"No, that's not all," I scolded her. "You have to have something to be frightened *about*. What is it?"

She shook her head, twisting that handkerchief again and looking down into her lap.

"Lora!" I snapped. "Look at me!"

She lifted her head, frightened. "Yes?"

"Now what is it you are frightened of? Is it something about the Hall?"

No response—simply mute agony in the blue eyes.

"Is it someone up there—Mrs. Venefica?" It was a shot in the dark, as they say.

For a moment, I thought the shot had hit home, but after a flash of tension, Lora came to life again and shook her head vehemently. "Oh, no! Mrs. Venefica is marvelous! She's the leader of our club! She's wonderful, Mrs. Hammond! Just simply wonderful!"

I sank back in my chair, observing the girl sharply. She simply could not communicate her inner feelings to me. It was extremely frustrating not to be able to get to the bottom of Lora's distress. There was no question but that she had been driven to the extremes of anxiety by *something*. The question remained—what was it?

Anxiety neurosis, I thought once again, my old text book phrases coming back to me after a few years' absence. The anxiety neurosis, I remembered, caused a person to be worried—anxious—perpetually, and not about one particular thing—a confrontation with a superior, for instance, or an appearance in front of a large number of people—but simply anxious about the *next moment in time*.

Was that Lora's problem? If so, she would have to be watched, to make sure it did not affect her adversely. Still, with compatible people like the girls on the fourth floor, perhaps Lora could be enticed out of her neurotic pattern and learn to make her way with them.

The trouble was, the background of Lora Blake was very sketchy. We had enrolled her at the Hall on the request of her uncle in California without actually knowing any details of her past in Illinois. Perhaps we should have. On the other hand, she was now here and it was too late for second guessing. It was up to the Hall—to me—to help her.

"If the people are nice, then what is bothering you?" I asked her in exasperation, hoping that my own open mood would stir her to reaction.

"I—I'm afraid—afraid to talk about the Bible that way." She sat slumped in her chair, and now her hands were still, and her body was almost flaccid in posture.

"The Bible!" I could not help echoing the word in surprise.

Her voice was low, and she would not look at me. "You think I'm a fool, the way *they* do. I was brought up very strictly," she said, her voice gaining strength as she went on. "And my mother and father told me that everything would always be all right if I did what the Bible said to do."

I blinked. There was no deep-seated problem here. Lora Blake, from a very strict religious home in the midwest, had come to a place where the girls were more worldly, more sophisticated, and more mature, and she had been shocked by what they said and did in her presence. Using the words "hell" and "damn." Saying "God" in a loose fashion. Lora Blake was simply reacting in a very normal way to being placed in a totally secular place after her protected youth.

"They don't mean it," I said in a low voice. "Lora, you believe in what you wish. Don't let them make fun of your beliefs. And don't let them see that you are hurt when they insult your faith. Do you understand me?"

She looked up at me with those pathetic eyes. "Yes, Mrs. Hammond."

"Then is that what you came to me for?"

She hesitated, looked about desperately, and then said: "Yes."

"Lora, I don't believe you!" I snapped. "Are you holding something back even now?"

"I'm not holding anything back!" she said breathlessly. "Please, Mrs. Hammond! I'm not holding anything back!"

I stared at her in dismay. She was almost in a frenzy, staggering out of her chair, and backing away to the door, reaching out for the knob, blindly, behind her, and wrenching the door open.

"It's all right, Mrs. Hammond! I'm not holding anything back!"

I stood to try to prevent her going, but she had already disappeared down the hallway when I gained the door.

I spoke to Mrs. Venefica in her stuffy little office that afternoon. Mrs. Venefica was as parchment-gray as always, and had the windows sealed tight so that the room itself seemed, once again, like a miniature greenhouse. I could smell the strange scent of something sharp and tangy in the air. I wondered what it could be.

But I refrained from asking.

"It's not often that you visit me, Mrs. Hammond," Mrs. Venefica said in that thin, threnodic voice of hers.

"It's not been necessary," I said with a smile. "But

now I am concerned about one of the girls on your floor."

"Ah?" Mrs. Venefica stared at me with a vacant look. "All my children are fine, I assure you, Mrs. Hammond. All!"

"It's Lora Blake I'm worried about," I said.

"Worried? Why are you worried about Lora?" Mrs. Venefica smoothed her dress down around her hips and straightened her shoulders. "She's a fine young girl."

"She's frightened," I said.

"Frightened of what?" Mrs. Venefica asked, her face innocent.

"She wouldn't tell me."

"Then she's simply making up stories." Mrs. Venefica sighed. "We've been trying to get Lora to stop that. She is a fantastic little fibber, you know, Mrs. Hammond!"

I watched Mrs. Venefica a moment in silence. She was very clever, Mrs. Venefica. She had given me the only kind of argument that I could not rebut. And she had given me an absolutely logical reason for the strange interview I had had with Lora.

"Do the girls like her?" I asked quickly.

"They love her!" Mrs. Venefica responded, clasping her hands and looking gleefully at the ceiling. "Ours is a beautiful family!"

"Will you please watch her carefully," I said, standing up to go. "I'm worried about her—even though I do understand about the tale-telling."

Mrs. Venefica stood up, too. "Oh, of course, Mrs. Hammond! I certainly will! I wouldn't want anything to happen to our happy little Lora! She's the youngest of us all, you know! And there's very special significance to the young, isn't there?"

I stared at her, and was on the verge of asking her a most extraordinary question, but at the last moment I could not force it out past my lips, and I desisted and turned to go.

As I reached out for the door knob I saw the plant in the pot on the wall nearby my shoulder *move*.

I wheeled and stared at Mrs. Venefica. She was

watching me with a clearly blank face—a face resembling a blackboard that had been wiped clean of all chalk marks.

I ran down the stairs.

Don had to stay in New York again that night. In the late afternoon he called me at the Hall. I decided to take the bus up to the nearest crossroads and walk to the house on Cold Brook Drive.

Before I left, Lora Blake drew me aside in the downstairs hall.

"I've got to see you alone, Mrs. Hammond!" she whispered, tears coming into her eyes.

"We're alone now," I said.

"Not *here*. I'm afraid—here!"

"Where?"

"At your home?"

"How will you get there?"

"I can always take a cab," she said tremulously.

She was much more worldly than I had been led to believe.

"Certainly. Come up tonight at eight o'clock. I'll be alone. My husband has to work." I gave her the address.

"Oh, thank you, Mrs. Hammond!"

And she was gone.

I waited until eight-thirty for her to come, but she did not. By ten I had given up on her, and at eleven I went to bed.

In the morning I ran into her.

"I waited for you, Lora. What happened?"

She stared at me blankly, her blue eyes unclouded. "I don't understand what you're talking about, Mrs. Hammond."

"You wanted to come to my house last night. Where were you?"

"I? I wanted to come see you?" Lora blinked rapidly. "But whatever for?"

"You were frightened."

"Frightened?" she repeated. "Of what?"

36

She was making a fool of me. "Where were you last night?" I asked her sharply.

"With the girls, of course." She smiled brightly.

"And you don't remember asking me to talk with you alone?"

"Of course not." She frowned. "I didn't, did I?"

I stared at her.

Something was all wrong here. She did not have enough imagination to lie. Mrs. Venefica was wrong. Or Mrs. Venefica was lying.

I turned on my heel, thinking that perhaps it was I who might be going slowly mad in this strange place.

I could hear soft laughter as I walked rapidly away from her.

Chapter Four

Suddenly the crisis at Don's company in New York evaporated and everything was back to normal. Don came home early a few times and began looking more human than he had during the long period of tension and pressure.

About three days after the break, he was sitting with me out in the back porch after dinner, just whiling away the time before going to bed. It was fun to be home and simply lolling around. I was glad that his work was going well.

So, for that matter, was mine.

"I've been meaning to ask you," Don said with a smile. "Have you had any more of those dreams you used to have?"

I hesitated. "What dreams, Don?"

"You know. Like that weird one. The one where you think you're burning up."

I spoke cautiously. "No, Don. I had it several times right after it first happened. But I haven't had it lately."

Actually, that was a bold-faced lie. But I had only had the dream two times within the past week—and that was far fewer times than I had had it the week before. The dream was becoming less virulent, even though it was by no means gone.

He made a noise in his throat.

I should have let the matter drop, but I could not. Don seemed somewhat more interested than he would ordinarily be. I wondered if there was something he had heard, or something about which he was worried. I suppose I was over-sensitive because of all the trouble Ben Magruder had given me about the pentacle at the Hall and the strange plants and music.

"Why do you ask, Don?"

He turned to look at me. We were sitting in the semi-darkness, but I could tell by his expression that he was studying me carefully. I also detected a reluctance in him to discuss the matter.

"I was just sitting here thinking about how excited Ben Magruder got when he heard about it here that first night."

"Oh, you know Ben!" I scoffed.

"But Ben's no fool, Aimee," Don said seriously.

Because of Don's preoccupation with work, I had not completely filled him in on the Lora Blake mystery, nor had I told him about what transpired at that second visit I had had from Ben Magruder—the discussion on the pentacle at the Hall. It was the first time I realized that Don did not know about the pentacle. I dreaded telling him now, and so I did not.

"Of course he's no fool," I said. "Well, what is it you want to talk about?"

He turned toward me, saying nothing.

"Come on, Don! I know you better than that. There's something you want to discuss. What is it?"

Don sank back into the chair and remained silent for about a minute. Finally, he nodded and said:

"All right. I think I had better tell you. It's one of those things best left unsaid, but I think circumstances warrant some kind of statement at this time, in view of Ben Magruder's interest in the matter."

"What—matter?" I asked, cautiously.

Don grinned. "It's going to sound pretty funny, so get ready to laugh, Aimee."

"I'm ready," I said. Somehow I did not feel like laughing at all. The memory of Ben Magruder's seriousness and his insistence on my leaving the Hall all came rushing back to me. I was annoyed at myself for not keeping Ben informed of the Lora Blake situation—which seemed one more point of proof for what Ben had been saying. And yet...

"I ran into Tom Denver on the train this afternoon," said Don leisurely, beginning to narrate one of his long-winded anecdotes. I remembered how I had always loved to ramble along with Don through his circumlocutions, his asides and his diversions on the way to the point of the talk, but now I realized I had become tense and irritable.

"Tom Denver? I don't remember him, do I?" I asked.

"We went to dinner with him and his wife once when we were in the Village," Don said. "You remember. That place on Barrow Street."

"Oh," I said. Then it came back to me. Yes. I remembered Tom Denver and his wife. He was a very small man—only five feet four, I believe—with an ego indirectly proportionate to his size.

His wife was a clam. She was pretty, a dark-eyed, dark-haired little thing, utterly feminine and totally dominated by Tom Denver's masculinity. Women like that give me a pain. I remembered her name. Ilene. Given other conditions, I am sure I would have liked her very much. But with Tom Denver dominating the conversation and the proceedings, I had simply closed my mouth and let the evening go along without me.

"Does he still wear a crew-cut?" I asked. If so, he would be the last crew-cut male in America.

Don looked irritated. "I forgot. You never did like Tom. Well, I do. I think he's a hell of a bright guy."

"Agreed," I sighed. "Now don't let me put you off. What happened when you met Tom Denver?" I could not help but think that this was all leading up to something vaguely connected with Ben Magruder and the Hall.

"We began talking. He lives up in Darien, you know. He said he and Ilene were expecting their first child."

I made appropriate sounds.

"But then he asked about you, and I told him you have a job at the Fairfield Residence Hall."

I watched Don and saw that he had stopped talking and was staring out into the deepening darkness of the back yard.

"Well?" I prompted him.

"I'm trying to get this all together in my head so I won't say anything wrong."

It all sounded very important.

Finally, Don began speaking. "Tom and Ilene have been in Darien for about two years now. They were living there when we met them in New York and had dinner with them." Don stopped to think some more. Then he went on. "When I mentioned the Hall, Tom became very alert and attentive to what I was saying."

I could picture that little pipsqueak sitting there and giving Don all his attention.

"What about the Hall?"

"Tom says he remembers it all so clearly because it happened the first week he and Ilene were living in Darien. The papers came out with this weird story, and Tom was assigned the piece for *Moment*."

I forgot to mention that Tom Denver worked in New York for the newsmagazine *Moment*.

"Did the story have anything to do with the Hall?"

"Let me get to that," Don said patiently. "When Tom was assigned the story, all that was known in Coldwater was that one of the girls living at the Hall was found garroted in the bushes just off the Merritt Parkway."

I could hear myself gasp. I had been expecting a great number of surprising things, but I had never expected anything so bizarre and gross as that!

"Garroted?" I repeated.

"Yeah," said Don, becoming very he-man, suddenly. He began to move his hands in pantomime. "You take a belt or a rope, twist each end around your wrists for a secure hold, and slip the piece of rope or belt over the head of the victim, wrap the two ends together—one, two, three—and you strangle the victim!"

I turned away. "Please, Don. You're so graphic."

He looked pleased. "Anyway, that was the story when Tom got into it."

"There's more?" I asked.

"You bet your life."

I subsided.

"Okay. The newspaper guys in Coldwater were on the story, and when Tom arrived with some members of the New York press, they began to badger the Chief of Police of Coldwater. One of the local newsmen had gotten a surreptitious look at the autopsy report and said he had seen some note to the effect that the victim had been drugged in some fashion before being garroted."

I was holding my breath.

"Tom said it was a very bizarre twist to the case, because usually garrotings are performed on rape victims because the victims are unwilling to submit to sexual inter—"

"Please, Don!" I cried. I had closed my eyes.

"All right. I'm sorry." Don sulked. "Anyway, the reporter had seen something, and because he had seen it, they all began to lean on the local Chief of Police. Finally the *Newsweek* guy got to the medical examiner through a relative of the M.E.'s, and found out that indeed the girl had ingested specific contents of an erotic mixture of herbs and plants that approximated a kind of hallucinogenic drug. Something like mescaline."

I sat up straight. "The Indians use that," I murmured.

"Right. And do you know, mescaline is a modern version of an ancient mixture of herbs and plants used in certain kinds of devil worship?"

I sank back into my chair, almost afraid to look at Don.

"Devil—worship?"

"That's right. Isn't that a spooky thing?"

"Yes," I admitted. "But—"

"There's more," said Don.

"Well then?"

"Finally, the medical examiner admitted to Tom Denver and several of the other reporters that a person could die from that kind of drug mixture, particularly if he or she were susceptible to certain kinds of allergies. I can't remember them at all, but Tom can recite them like the alphabet."

I nodded.

"Anyway, they never did catch the murderer, and the case is, to this day, unsolved." Don looked over at me, triumphantly.

"It all sounds rather far-fetched. Like something a reporter would make up for a good story."

Don was sarcastic. "You mean the kind of story a no-good like Tom Denver would dream up to make points with the boss?"

"Exactly," I snapped back.

Silence.

"Well, there's more, Aimee," Don said in a low voice.

"More?"

"About six months after that, another girl from the Hall hit the newspapers. Because of the earlier case of the garroted girl at the Hall, the New York papers were onto it immediately. And so was Tom Denver."

"Another garroting?" I asked in astonishment.

"No. This was the case of a girl who appeared suddenly, in the dead of night, at the front door of the Coldwater Police Station, dressed only in her nightgown, and insisted on being put under police protection."

"Protection against what?" I asked.

"She said someone was trying to burn her alive!" Don answered in a soft voice.

"Burn her alive!" I could hardly get the words out. How well I knew that feeling! The flames, the heat, the essence of evil stifling you, preventing you from breathing! And the heat—the heat! But it was only a dream! Nothing real! Why should I feel this deadly fear? Nonsense! I told myself. Forget this silly feeling! It is all in the imagination.

"She kept telling the police over and over that she was being burned alive, that someone had given her some poison to consume her."

"What—what happened?"

"The police tried to hold her for awhile, questioned the head of the Hall, but found no basis for suspicion of any kind, and finally referred the girl to the county home."

"Oh?

"Ten days later she died."

I could not speak.

"During the entire time she was at the county home, she kept telling everyone who would listen that she was burning alive. She pleaded with them to put out the flames, to save her life, but no one could help her. They thought she was mad, of course."

"How did she die?"

"Drowned, actually. Somehow she escaped from her room, where she was being held, and jumped into the rather large pond out in back of the home. She simply went down into the water and drowned. They found her body next morning floating in the pond."

I shook my head helplessly, and could feel my skin creeping along my flesh.

"At the autopsy, the medical examiner found that she was completely normal."

"No drugs?" I asked.

"No evidence of anything unusual," Don said.

"Then that proves it! Nothing happened to her. She

43

was simply making it up about the burning! She was half-crazy and—"

"Aimee! I think you missed the point. She said she was burning up! Isn't that exactly what you dreamed right after you went to work there?"

I stared at Don and felt the breath being squeezed out of my chest.

"Well, wasn't it?" he persisted.

"Yes," I said, finally. "But that's just a nightmare! You know that's all it is." Yes! It was all in my imagination—nowhere else!

"That's why I'm glad you don't dream that one any more," Don said flatly.

"Yes," I said.

His eyes searched my face in the darkness. "You *don't* dream it any more, do you?"

"You should know!" I said, triumphantly.

"The—the sex antics?" he asked with a gentle smile. "But that never happened again, Aimee. You know that was only the first time. The other times the dream was simply a nightmare."

"You see?"

He sank back in the chair, musing. "It doesn't matter. Even if the dreams have stopped, I don't want you working at that place, Aimee."

"You don't want me working there?" I cried, astonished. "Don—am I hearing you right?"

"Yes," he snapped. "You certainly are! That place is some kind of a crazy house! Witchcraft. Dreams of burning up. Spooks. I'd swear there is something wrong with it! Ben Magruder never did like it. He didn't say anything about it, but he didn't have to. I could tell by the look on his face!"

I played innocent. I knew that Don was going to be stubborn about this. Rarely did he interfere in my own aims and hopes. We had agreed not to argue with each other about our professional plans before we had married. But I knew that now he was going to. And I did not know how to counteract it.

"If it's all that important, why don't you call Ben Magruder?"

He looked at me and frowned. "He'd think I was a fool. I'm sure he knows about those deaths!"

Certainly he must have heard about them. But he had not told me of them because he knew it would frighten me. And since I was stubborn and insisted on keeping on the job at the Hall, he knew that if he frightened me, I would be even more insistent on staying. He had all my quirks of character figured out right, and he acted on them.

"I think it's all a lot of nonsense—something made up by Tom Denver!"

"It wasn't made up by Tom Denver. But even if it was, and even if none of this were true, I've decided at this point that I don't want you working there, Aimee."

"Oh, you don't!" I said, beginning to bridle.

"No, I don't! Now don't get argumentative with me, Aimee! I've put up with it for several months now, but only because I've been busy. I have to admit that when I went down to that creep joint the night of the October Social, I didn't like it one bit. I've never seen so many creepy girls and weird women together in one place. And that crazy nut on the fourth floor—that Mrs. Venefica—she's enough to drive an ordinary person up the wall!"

"She's a harmless old lady," I rejoined with spirit. "And she's lonely and frightened and needs the company of the girls."

"She's got tendencies I wouldn't want to think about," snapped Don dryly. "I've had it with the place, Aimee. Even if you haven't. I want you to quit."

"I won't quit."

He stared at me. "You're as stubborn as a mule, you know that, Aimee? They should call you Jennie!"

"I'm not being stubborn. I'm being sensible. You come home with a lot of gibberish that I don't believe, and try to order me to quit my job! Are you jealous, Don? Don't you want me to make money too? Is there something about my working that makes you envious?"

"Don't be a fool, Aimee" he said, but I could hear by the tone of his voice that he was backing down.

"I won't quit! I'll work there even if it is a weird place, which I don't believe for one moment!"

"And keep on dreaming the dreams?"

"And keep on——" I said, and then realized that he had trapped me. "How did you know I was still having those dreams?" I asked in a low voice.

He moved toward me. "Because last night was exactly like the first night, Aimee. I didn't wake you up, but you were all over me. It was as if you were somebody else again." He eyed me a moment. "I don't like it, Aimee. I want you out of there. I really am beginning to fear for your sanity."

"You can't be serious!"

"I can be and I am being serious."

I stood up and walked about the porch a moment. I wanted to clear my head. For some reason, I found it difficult to think. I had been quite cool and now I was suddenly hot. It was as if a fever had begun to burn in me.

And with the fever came a lack of concentration. I could not really think clearly. I knew that I should be thinking about the Hall, and about the dream I had been having, but I could not put the thoughts together. My mind was exactly like a broken mirror—all the pieces pointing in different directions.

"Aimee?" Through the confusion inside and outside me, I could hear Don's voice.

"Yes?"

"What's the matter?"

I shook my head and closed my eyes, but the ache in my head and the confusion in my brain remained.

"Nothing," I said mechanically.

He was holding me close to him. I knew that he would not probe further if I kissed him. I did. He responded. I had never used his love that way before, but that night I did. We went to bed early. And I do not remember what happened; I only know that I was wanton, once again—not Aimee at all, but some look-alike from the opposite side of the sky. I closed my mind against it.

And he did not mention the Hall again that night.

Chapter Five

All the next day, I remember wandering around the Hall in a particularly listless manner, as if I were too tired to know what I was doing. I seemed to have exhausted myself completely. Or perhaps I was coming down with some kind of bug.

I simply did not care.

During lunch hour, I lay on one of the cots upstairs and dozed briefly, only to be awakened by a recurrence of the burning dream. I was soaked with perspiration as I blundered out into the hallway.

To my astonishment I found myself on the fourth floor; I had certainly not climbed to the top of the Hall just to rest! And yet, of course, I must have done so.

Blundering out into the hall, my eyes half-closed, and my head throbbing, I moved over toward the stairway near Mrs. Venefica's office.

As I passed one of the closed doors, I heard the chanting. I call it chanting, because that was exactly what it sounded like to me: the chanting of a number of voices.

I stopped by the door and listened.

So groggy was I from sleep, or so confused was I from fatigue, that I could hardly make out the words. Or perhaps it is that I imagined them. But this is what I thought I heard at the time:

"Keimi, Keimi, I am the Great One, in whose mouth rests Kommona, Thoth, Naumbre, Karikha, Kenyryo, Paarminathon, the sacred Ian Ienacoi, who is above the heaven."

Astounded, I leaned against the door and put my ear to it to hear more. It sounded to me as if there were at least a dozen girls in there, all chanting in a very low voice, these strange words—words that seemed to be part of some dreadfully secret ritual:

"I named thy glorious name, the name for all needs. Put thyself in connection with us, O hidden one, God, with respect to us, which Apollogex also used."

For a long moment, I leaned there against the door, listening to my heart bang against my ribs. I thought of Tom Denver's story of the weird goings on at the Hall and I thought of Ben Magruder's insistence that I get out of there once and for all, and I thought of Don's plea with me to leave.

I thought suddenly that I *must* go—that there was indeed some strange, sinister business going on here at the Hall! Ben Magruder was not mistaken; there was a witch practicing here. And what I had heard was a witch cult making some kind of demand of the Devil. Even though they called the Devil "God," it was obvious what these practitioners were.

It came to me that Lora Blake might have good reason to fear for her soul in an atmosphere like this. Now I knew why she was worried about her faith in God. Certainly, if her peers were all worshipping the Devil, they would not have kind things to say about God!

I closed my eyes. I was wearier than I had been for days. I remained there a moment, simply leaning against the door.

When I stirred again I pressed my ear against the door but could hear nothing.

Yet I knew there was someone in there. Perhaps they had heard me eavesdropping and were remaining silent so I would go away.

I grasped the knob of the door angrily and thrust it open, trying to see who was in the room. I would remember each name and—

The room was deserted.

I knew now that it was Cindy Loomis's room. It was small—the kind of typical cell the Hall had for its girls—and certainly twelve people would have a great deal of trouble fitting into it.

Apparently, I had imagined the whole thing.

I stood staring there at the empty room and frowning. I was tired now, overwhelmingly tired, and I needed rest.

As I was about to pull the door shut I saw the rug on the floor. It was one of those bright-colored throw rugs that had been woven into a kind of Indian pattern. I stared at it, and I saw there was a lot of red and yellow and orange in the pattern.

Hypnotized almost, I stepped forward and lifted the rug quickly from the floor. A pentacle?

There was nothing under the rug and I replaced it shame-facedly. What kind of idiocy was I fantasizing? I had let Ben Magruder's imagination run away with me—that was the answer.

Who was Keimi? I wondered. Thoth? Wasn't that a god of Ancient Egypt? Or perhaps not. And if there were not people in that room now, how could I ever prove there had been someone in there before?

I closed the door and turned to face down the corridor. My eyes were slightly unfocused, and as I began to walk forward I felt that I might fall flat on my face.

There was a tiny window set high in the wall at the end of the hallway where the stairs turned to go down just outside Mrs. Venefica's office, and I paused there, trying to steady my legs.

Casually, I glanced through the small window out into the street. It was very bright out—a brilliant, autumn day—and I could see people walking by on the sidewalk and cars moving up and down the street.

Stunned, I stared at the figure in front of the Hall. He was standing there on the sidewalk, hands on his hips, and looking up right at me, as if he had commanded me to appear there!

It was Ben Magruder!

My indecision and confusion vanished.

I started down the stairs. At the same moment, I could hear the crash of something falling inside Mrs. Venefica's office. I hesitated an instant on the stairs, torn between two courses of action: rushing out to see Ben, and rushing back to see what had happened in Mrs. Venefica's office. I guessed that it was she who had been leading that group of girls in that secret rite. But I could never prove it. Perhaps something in her office ...

And yet Ben's expression had been one of urgency.

I rushed down and out into the street.

He stared at me with relief.

"Aimee! You're all right?"

"Yes, of course," I said, even though I still felt weak and peaked.

"You're looking rather pale, my dear," he said, touching me with kindly hands. He glanced about and pointed to a concrete bench outside the bookstore, next door. "Let's sit down."

"Ben, I've an awful lot to do. I really should get back."

"Nonsense!" he snorted. "I came all the way down here to talk—*and we're going to talk!*"

I moved docilely with him to the concrete bench and we sat.

"Don called me," he said without preamble.

"He had no right to do that!" I snapped.

"He had all the right in the world, Aimee," said Ben firmly. "You're a fool not to have told me yourself."

"Gossipy little man," I muttered.

"You're talking about that friend of Don's on the train, I presume," Ben said with a faint smile. "Don said you didn't like him. Therefore, you wouldn't like what he had to say."

I stiffened and turned to look at Ben Magruder. "Well?"

"The truth of the matter is that Don's friend was absolutely right. I looked up the records myself this morning after Don called."

"And?" I was feeling a little less annoyed now. In spite of myself, I was becoming interested.

"Everything Don told you is true. A girl did die by garroting. Her stomach was pumped out at autopsy.

And a weird combination of particles was found in her stomach."

"Indeed," I said stiffly.

Ben Magruder ticked them off on his fingers. "Annamthol. Betel. Opium. Cingfoil. Henbane. Belladonna. Hemlock. Cannabis Indica. Canthreindin."

I stared at him. "Opium? It was a drug, then?"

He shook his head. "Belladonna is a deadly poison, but in the small proportion found in the girl's stomach, it is also used as an hallucinogen. So is the henbane, the betel, the annamthol, the hemlock, and the cannabis."

"Marijuana?"

"Actually, hashish. Marijuana is *Cannabis Sativa*. There is very little difference, actually. It is the hemp plant, grown for its use as twine in ropes."

"The girl was a drug addict?" I asked.

"Not at all. She had simply ingested a witch's ointment used by practioners to induce strange hallucinations and 'visions.'"

I could think of nothing to say.

"And the other girl did drown herself, Aimee, because she could not rid herself of that recurring dream of burning alive."

"Ben Magruder," I said, "if you've persuaded me to sit with you and listen to this nonsense just because you're going to tell me to get out of that place, I've had enough for now!"

I stood up.

"Aimee, please," he said. "Sit down!"

I shook my head.

"You must consider your own safety!" he said.

I started to walk away. "I'm sorry, Ben. It's simply idiotic to talk about."

Ben came to his feet and started to follow me. "Please, Aimee. I promised Don—"

I wheeled on him angrily. "Promised him what?"

He stared at me. Neither of us moved. "I'm sorry, Aimee, I didn't mean to bring that up, but—"

"You promised him to get me to quit my job at the Hall, didn't you?"

Ben blinked in dismay.

"Neither one of you have any right to try to dominate me, Ben! Neither of you has the right to put me down that way! I'll do what I please, and I'll do it *when* I please! It suits me fine to stay at the Hall for the rest of my life, if I want to, and neither you nor Don can stop me!"

Ben Magruder was watching me with a despairing expression. He had folded his arms stubbornly over his chest. That made me all the more angry.

"And don't stand there looking so holier than thou! I'm my own boss, and I'm going to do what I want. You and your strange stories won't make me change my mind! You hear me?"

"Yes," said Ben softly. "I hear you."

"Good! Then I'm going! I'm sorry you wasted your time coming here to talk to me. Tell Don it was an unsuccessful foray!"

Ben sighed.

I spun on my heel and hurried along the sidewalk and up the stairs of the Hall.

As I did so I glanced upward and saw the curtain in Mrs. Venefica's office window move just the slightest.

But for the moment I was too angry to think what that might mean.

My rage had cleared my head and I felt better. As a matter of fact, the dizziness and confusion of the morning was all gone now.

I worked through the next few hours with a definite purpose in mind and a clear knowledge of everything that was going on about me.

It was four-thirty when Mrs. Venefica had her "spell".

She had just invited me in for a cup of tea with her, and in absolute rejection of everything Ben Magruder stood for, I agreed wholeheartedly to go.

Once again, I was oppressed by the smell in her office. That is, there was so heavy an odor of plant life and a kind of animal ripeness that I could barely breathe.

She closed the door and then it was unbearable. However, after a moment she got the tea pot going and came back to sit opposite me. She was smiling as always, and I felt like Gretel in *Hansel and Gretel*.

"You haven't been visiting me very much, Aimee," the old woman cackled as I sat there nervously.

"I've been terribly busy, Mrs. Venefica," I said.

"Not too busy to visit our fourth floor for a little rest, though," she said with a shrewd look at me.

I could feel my cheeks turning red. "Yes, I will admit I was tired this noon, but—"

"You should have come to me and told me you were tired. I'd have *fixed* you something."

My mind went absolutely blank. And then, in a twinkling, I thought of Ben Magruder and the list of exotic drugs that had been found in the garroted girl's stomach. I began to shake in my chair.

Mrs. Venefica noticed me. "Oh, is it too cold for you in here, my dear? That's strange. Someone else—I believe it was that wonderful little Lora Blake—complained about the heat in here this morning. I just don't know what the younger generation is coming to!" She smiled at me slyly.

"I'm far too warm," I said. "Please, Mrs. Venefica, perhaps the tea wasn't a good idea."

"No, it's a beautiful idea!" she crowed, and reached for the kettle which she emptied into a ceramic teapot on her desk. I could see the steam rising through the vents in the top of the pot. She had obviously loaded it with tea leaves before.

"A little mixture of my own," she told me as she lifted the pot and poured a cup of tea for me.

I took the cup she pushed at me and watched her lift her own to her lips. Our eyes met. She smiled. "Drink it down, Aimee," she said, and began to giggle.

I was frightened, very frightened. I could hear Ben Magruder's warning voice once again: "Get out of there, Aimee, for fear of your life!"

I lifted the teacup to my lips and the scent went into my nose.

It was like no other tea I had ever smelled!

I held the cup there, wondering what I should do with it. If I drank it, I had no idea what would happen. If I did not, Mrs. Venefica could choose some other way to make me drink her potions—whatever they were.

"Who's Keimi?" I asked quite suddenly, the question coming out of the blue.

"Keimi?" Mrs. Venefica repeated, smiling a frozen smile.

"Keimi. Kommona. Thoth."

Her eyes slid up into her skull. I was staring in consternation, and I watched the cup of tea spill out of her limp hand, and the cup smash to the floor and break into a thousand pieces, and Mrs. Venefica slump down lifelessly in her chair, and then slowly turn to one side and fall to the floor.

I was unable to move at first. I stared at my tea. I threw it from me with a violent gesture. Then I leaned down over Mrs. Venefica and felt her pulse.

There was none. None that I could feel.

I grabbed at the doorknob to open the door.

It would not open.

The heat and the oppressiveness of the room suddenly squeezed in on me and I felt like screaming.

In fact, I did scream.

"Let me out! I'm in Mrs. Venefica's room! Let me out!"

And I banged against the door, trying feebly to open it, but it would not open.

"Let me out of here!" I sobbed hysterically. "Let me out—I'm—I'm burning up—"

And indeed I was burning up, just like in that dream.

Someone called to me from the corridor.

"Mrs. Hammond! What's the matter?"

"I can't—"

But I could. I was grasping the doorknob. It turned and I was standing there in the open doorway looking embarrassed.

Lora Blake watched me from the corridor, puzzled.

"It's Mrs. Venefica!" I said, recovering quickly. "She's fainted—or had a heart attack—or something."

Pandemonium.

Before I knew what was happening, Mrs. Grant had gotten on the telephone and called for the doctor who treated Mrs. Venefica, from time to time. In a few minutes Dr. Kingsley came in, a tall, graying, no-nonsense man with a crisp manner and an assured air—the kind of man who reeks of family and of money—and he had Mrs. Venefica back on her feet in less than a minute.

I watched him as he came out of Mrs. Venefica's office. I could tell by his expression that he did not like the smell of the room, although he said nothing about it.

"How is she?" I asked.

He looked at me. I saw that his eyes were gray and piercing. He set down his bag a moment and smiled at me.

"She's perfectly all right. And you are—?"

"Mrs. Hammond. Aimee Hammond," I said.

"I see."

"I work for Mrs. Grant. I'm her assistant."

He nodded. "Well, Aimee," he said, "you just have to bear along with Mrs. Venefica. She is not young, and her body is playing tricks on her. It's a sad thing."

"A heart attack?"

He shook his head. "Actually, I have no idea what it is. But it's happened before. And when I give her a shot of—" he hesitated—"she seems to come out of it all right." He smiled. "When the body begins to go to pieces, it is difficult to pinpoint the exact locus of the trouble."

"I'm glad she's better," I said, for lack of anything else to say.

We were alone in the hallway at the moment. He peered at me. "Are you all right?"

I was startled. "All right? Of course I'm all right."

"You look a bit tired. Pale. Washed-out. You have a doctor, haven't you? I'd suggest you see him."

55

"But, Doctor—"
He was gone.

I made a mistake and told Don that night what Dr. Kingsley had said to me. I treated it as a joke, but Don did not.

"He's right, Aimee! That place is doing something to you. You should see Doctor Gainsborough."

"He's in New York, Don!"

"See him!" snapped Don. "I'll make an appointment."

But the next day Don phoned from New York and told me that Dr. Gainsborough had retired and was living in the Virgin Islands.

"Go see the doctor you talked to," he ordered me. "I'm serious, Aimee. Something is wrong with you!"

Reluctantly, I tried to reach Dr. Kingsley, only to find that he would not take any new patients. However, he was willing to talk to me and then refer me to someone else.

I thanked him, made an appointment with his nurse, and hung up.

He was every inch the suave sophisticate in his office as he had been in the hallway outside Mrs. Venefica's room.

"A physician does not go out of his way to solicit patients," he told me with a faint smile. "I apologize for what I said to you. However, it seems obvious to me that something is troubling you. Is there anything?"

"Physical?" I asked, sparring with him.

His eyes narrowed. "Let's not say necessarily. Are you troubled *mentally*?"

I sighed. I had to tell him. "A dream." I described it.

He frowned throughout my explanation, and when I had finished, he looked up thoughtfully.

"There's something in it," he said slowly. "A recurring dream *does* signify something disturbing psychologically."

"Then—?"

"I have a very good friend, a colleague, named Dr.

Strachey. He is an analyst. I think he should take a look at you. At least, a talk with him might be helpful."

"A psychoanalyst?" I repeated, thinking of the money.

"Oh, it's expensive. But I think he will recognize your youth and make concessions."

I rose. "All right, then, if you think I should."

"Indeed, I do think you should," he stressed, and walked me to the door of his office. "I'll give you his number."

I steeled myself to tell Don that night, but when it came right down to the actual words, I could not get them out.

He forgot to ask me if I had seen Dr. Kingsley. Some new crisis had arisen at the office, and it kept him occupied throughout dinner and into the evening.

Chapter Six

We were in bed, both asleep, when the pounding started on the front door. Don was the first to rouse himself. He was mumbling under his breath when I came awake, and reaching out for his trousers on the chair.

It took me a moment or two to orient myself, and I realized that I had been sleeping very deeply and calmly for most of the night. Now it was three o'clock—I could see that by the clock at my bedside.

Who was making that frantic racket?

I saw Don going through the door, shambling in that sleepwalker's way of his, and I pushed him aside and got to the front door before him. It took me only a moment to see that the person on the front porch was someone I knew and not a stranger.

"Come in, Lora!" I called to her, opening the door.

She was wild-eyed and disheveled, her hair hanging down over her face and shoulders, her face without make-up, her lips pale and white, her clothes thrown on haphazardly.

She turned to wave to the taxicab parked in front of the house, and it slowly drove off.

Don stood in the middle of the living room, blinking his eyes against the light, and trying to be debonair. It was no time for old-world manners. I took her over to the couch and made her sit down.

"What's the matter?" I asked. "What happened?"

Lora Blake simply shuddered and put her face in her hands.

Don paced up and down.

"Lora!" I called to her.

Finally, she looked up and her eyes focused on me. They were bright and wild. "Yes?"

"What happened?"

"I can't explain it! I can't!"

Don stopped pacing and stared at the girl. By now I had had time to sit back and take stock of Lora Blake's condition. She was on the brink of hysteria. I had seen that look before in some of my charges—not at the Hall—and I knew that she must be soothed and calmed for the time being until she could get out whatever piece of news she had.

"Try," said Don sternly.

She looked up at him, hang-dog and frightened.

I took her by the shoulder. "Is it something to do with the Hall? Is that why you took a cab from there?"

"Yes," she said in a trembling voice. "Something..."

"What?" I asked.

"It's the—the—rituals."

I glanced up at Don. He lifted an eyebrow.

"Rituals?"

"It's more than the rites," she said, starting to talk

now. "It's the way they've taken over my whole mind! Do you know what I mean?"

"I'm afraid I don't," I said.

Lora looked down and held her head. She did not attempt to speak again.

"What rites?" I asked gently.

"The rituals," she said with a sob.

"How do they go?" I asked, glancing up at Don to keep him from interrupting.

"I can't *remember*!" cried Lora. "That's what makes it so scary! I know there were rituals, but I can't remember anything!"

"Lora," I said, getting closer to her and holding her tightly now. "If you can't remember, then how do you know the rites have anything to do with your—your trouble?"

"Because it's my mind," said Lora, looking up at me wide-eyed. It was almost as if her eyes were empty, too, as well as her mind. "They're trying to take over my mind!"

From the recesses of my memory came the information I sought: invasion of the mind as a typical symptom of paranoia.

Lora, a paranoid? If not already, I reasoned, she was close to it.

"How?" I asked.

"I wake up sometimes and I don't know where I am. I don't know who I am," she said.

I nodded. "But then you do remember, don't you?"

"Yes. But sometimes I have to go to sleep first."

"Then they're not taking over your mind, really, are they? Because you always get it back."

"But sometime they'll make me lose my mind and I'll never get it back!" She began weeping.

"Who do you think 'they' are?" I asked.

Through her sobs she got the words out. "I think it's the girls."

"Which girls?"

"The girls on the fourth floor, of course. And that old Mrs. Venefica."

There was silence for a moment. Don sat down opposite us and looked at me through narrowed eyes.

"Let's have it from the beginning. The rituals, Lora."

Sniffling, she lifted her head. "They invited me in the first day I was at the Hall, you know," she said. "And they told me that they were playing games and that I must join them. I did. They began singing and chanting and then sitting around in a circle and—and making mysterious passes and drawing weird signs on the floor."

"Witch cult," said Don softly from across the room. Ben Magruder was right!"

"Yes," said Lora, surprisingly. "There are twelve of us, and Mrs. Venefica. You see? But—" Silence.

"But what, Lora?"

"It's all in fun. There's nothing to it. It has nothing to do with this—this other thing!"

"What other thing?"

"Taking my mind away!"

"You're saying now it has nothing to do with the rituals?"

"I don't think so. No. The circle of magic is a joke—a game we play. Sure, I'm religious, like I told you, Mrs. Hammond, and they tease me, but it doesn't bother me now. I got used to it. And the demonology game, it was just a game. I'm all over that. Even the girls got tired of that."

Don stared across at Lora. "Then what is it?"

"I don't know," Lora whispered softly, putting her hands around her head and closing her eyes. "Something is trying to break into my head and steal my mind."

"But it sounds exactly like the circle of magic has gotten you into its power," I said. "Are you sure it isn't the girls?"

"I don't know anymore!" cried Lora. "But I think not. After all, that's only a game!"

Her eyes were pleading.

"What do you want to do, Lora?" I asked, rising and going across the room toward the kitchen.

"I don't know," she said sadly.

I heated water in the kettle and got the teapot ready.

Don was chatting with her when I got back with the tea.

"How did you get away from the Hall?" Don asked casually.

"I put on my clothes, grabbed up what little money I had, and ran outside."

"Did anyone follow you?"

Lora frowned. "I think not. Anyway, I hailed a cab down near the railroad station and had the cabbie bring me out to your house. You were the only person I could trust, Mrs. Hammond."

I smiled. "Here's some tea for you, Lora. It'll steady your nerves. Then you can go back to the Hall and forget about this nightmare."

She was shaking, her face white. "I'll never go back!"

"But you can't stay here!" I cried.

"I don't want to," Lora admitted, "but I've got to get away from here. I'm frightened, Mrs. Hammond."

"Do you have any relatives?" Don asked.

"In California," Lora answered after a moment, letting the hot tea warm her up. "Perhaps you could take me to the airport where I could see about getting on a plane."

Don nodded. "No problem, I'll get the car out and drive you to Kennedy right now. If you're reluctant to go back to the Hall, there's no sense in going there. Your things can be sent out later."

"Do you think going to California will solve the problem?" I asked cautiously.

Lora stared at me, wide-eyed. "Why shouldn't it?"

"Perhaps you will be taking the problem along with you," I suggested.

"But it's the Hall, Mrs. Hammond! It's the place! It's—it's—full of witches!"

Don laughed.

Lora drew away from him and looked down at the cup in her hand. She was shaking again. I was sorry for her, and I was angry at Don for upsetting her with that masculine and contemptuous laugh of his.

"He didn't mean to hurt your feelings," I said.

She said nothing.

I turned to Don. "I'll take her to the airport, dear. While we're gone, why don't you telephone ahead to get her a reservation."

Don looked up at me with a funny smile. *"I'll* drive her there."

"No. I will!"

"Oh, Aimee! Stop it now. You sound just like a woman's libber."

"Don, I'll drive her down. I want you to stay here."

"No way," said Don. "Wait here while I get dressed, and we'll go together to Kennedy Airport."

Don hastened out of the room and I heard him close the door and start dressing.

I slipped quickly into a raincoat that fit tightly over my robe and got the keys to the car out of my bag. With my finger to my lips for silence, I took Lora by the hand and tiptoed out of the house.

I was backing out of the driveway when I saw Don at the door, waving his hands frantically and shouting to us.

I turned in the street and headed for the Merritt Parkway.

Beside me Lora settled down with her eyes closed and before we had gone a mile or two, she was asleep.

I paid my first toll on the Merritt Parkway, and that was the last thing I remembered.

The next thing I knew I was sitting in my living room with the light on.

I thought back, and could only remember paying that toll. Then nothing. Except the burning sensation. The burning and the nightmarish sounds.

The bedroom door burst open angrily.

Don stood there in his pajamas, trembling with rage. "That's the last time I let you get away with anything like that, Aimee!" he said in a determined voice. "You hear me?"

"I hear you," I said softly.

He subsided somewhat. "Well, did you get her to the airport?"

I looked at him. How could I tell him I did not know if I had even gotten to the airport?

"Yes," I said, looking away. "I'm tired, Don. Shall we go to bed?"

"Of course!" he said angrily. "It's five-thirty. But don't think I'm going to forgive you quite so easily!"

I walked over to him and stood in front of him. I lifted my mouth and kissed him firmly. He laughed deep in his throat, and grabbed me and I was forgiven.

He let me off at the Hall after breakfast and I went in still trying to remember what had happened on the Merritt Parkway the night before when I had blacked out.

I thought of it as "blacking out." I had no idea what had really happened. But now I could remember that I had endured that burning sensation once again. When? I did not know, but I assumed it must have been just after the moment I had blacked out. The dream? The nightmare?

But why did I draw a blank about driving on to New York and putting Lora Blake on the plane?

I had no idea.

Mrs. Grant greeted me, and I smiled and went about my work. However, I had not gotten through an hour of it when I realized that I could not keep my mind on what I was doing. I was dazed, really, as if exhausted from some strange malady.

Because my mind was in such a turmoil, I cannot remember much about that day at all. I know that once in the afternoon I almost telephoned Don at his office to confess to him that I was not sure whether or not I had delivered Lora Blake to the airport. But I knew that the first thing he would ask me was: where was Lora? And I did not know the answer to that question at all.

Like a sleepwalker, I went through my daily routine and finally finished up and went back to my office to sit down a moment to unwind.

I was seated there, mute and dazed, with the door half-open, staring into space and wishing the day were finished so Don would come by to pick me up, when I saw a girl walk by the office, going toward the kitchen.

The girl was Lora Blake!

Stunned, I rose from my seat and started for the doorway.

"Lora!" I called, reaching out unconsciously as if to halt her, even though she was far beyond my reach.

She halted and turned to regard me.

Her eyes were blank and only half-focused.

"Yes, Mrs. Hammond?"

"Lora," I whispered, choking on the name. "Whatever—whatever *happened*?"

"Happened, Mrs. Hammond?"

I was in the hallway now, and she was staring at me as if totally unaware of what I was talking about.

"Last night, Lora," I said in a low voice, glancing about to make sure no one was eavesdropping.

"Last night, Mrs. Hammond?" she repeated blankly.

"The house," I said urgently. "The airport! You know? The trip to California?"

Lora smiled. "You're teasing me, Mrs. Hammond. What trip to California?"

"Lora," I said swiftly, "don't you have relatives in California?"

"Yes," she said vaguely. "But—"

"You wanted to leave the Hall and visit them last night! And you came to my house. I took you to the airport. Why are you back?"

"Your house, Mrs. Hammond?" She smiled blankly. "How could I come to your house?"

I swallowed hard.

"You're implying to me that you did not come to my house last night in a cab?"

Lora Blake laughed. "I've never taken a taxicab in Coldwater in my life!"

I was momentarily unable to continue. But then I managed to rally myself a bit.

"Where were you last night?"

"Asleep in my room," she said innocently.

"And the rites?"

Lora blinked. "Rites? What rites?"

"The magic rituals," I said impatiently. "We talked about it last night."

"There are no magic rituals," Lora smiled with amusement. "Are you trying to put me on, Mrs. Hammond?"

I gripped her arm hard so that I knew it hurt. "Now you listen to me, Lora! Tell me the truth! How did you get back to the Hall?"

"I never left the Hall, Mrs. Hammond," said Lora angrily, wrestling herself from me. "And take your hand away. You're hurting me!"

I let her go as if she were on fire. "You're lying, Lora!" I snapped.

She stiffened, and I knew that I had hurt her feelings badly. In her conscious mind she did not remember what had happened. I could see that now. Therefore, she must have been in some kind of trance or in some state of extreme agitation of which she had no recall at all.

"I'm sorry, Mrs. Hammond. I do have to get back to my room. If you please?"

I waved her off, annoyed with myself for losing my temper.

Lora Blake went off in the direction of the kitchen. I went back to the office and sat there, trying to think. But my mind was moving about in a kaleidoscope of fantasies, colors, musical sounds, and shapes.

I could not concentrate!

I was still sitting there when I heard the scream. It seemed to come from far off, but then it was repeated and I knew that it was in the building.

A scream?

Lethargically, I stirred myself, and moved out into the hallway, looking up the stairway, for the scream had come from the upper regions of the building.

Someone called to me from the hall, but I paid no attention. Instead, I was on my way up those stairs. I did not even have to think. I knew that the person who had screamed was Lora Blake!

She had gone up the stairs to her room and she was up there and she was screaming!

I was running now, trying to take the stairs three at a time, but not succeeding. And I could see several others following me far back.

The scream came again.

"Help me!"

And I tried to accelerate my pace, but it was an agony of effort to get up that last flight of stairs to the fourth floor.

"Help me!" the cry came again.

It was Lora Blake.

I saw Mrs. Venefica's door. It was closed. And as I started past it, I heard the scream again, and it came from inside Mrs. Venefica's room.

"Help!"

I grasped the doorknob and pulled it open. This time it did not stick.

Two people were inside the room, and for one crazy instant I thought I saw Mrs. Venefica struggling with Lora Blake next to an open window. Open window? Mrs. Venefica never had a window open that I had seen. She always kept herself inside that hothouse with no ventilation at all, so her plants would have good growing conditions.

Yet ...

It was not Mrs. Venefica. It was Jill Towers, the girl who did the typing. She was struggling with Lora Blake. I did not stop to wonder how they had gotten into Mrs. Venefica's room, but pushed past the crowded desk and tried to reach Lora Blake.

"Help me!" screamed Lora Blake.

"Don't!" cried Jill Towers.

Lora Blake swung around, and slammed her elbow into Jill's jaw. Jill fell back and crashed into the crowded desk. Two flower pots fell off and smashed on the floor. There was a strange earthy stench in the air.

Lora stared wide-eyed at Jill as she slumped to the floor, took one bright-eyed look at me, and then grabbed the frame of the open window, climbed onto the sill, poised there for one brief moment as I vainly tried to cross the room to grab her, and jumped.

"Lora!" I screamed.

The door behind me was pushed hard and a group of girls were behind me, staring open-mouthed at the empty window.

Jill Towers slowly rose from where she had been thrown by the fury of Lora's attack, and rubbed her chin with her hand. Tears were in her eyes.

I leaped for the window and stared down into the small garden that bordered the sidewalk.

I was sick.

It was Lora Blake.

She was suspended, face down, on the small wrought-iron picket fence, with one of the heavy iron spikes protruding from her back. Blood was seeping out around the rusty iron.

I turned away from the window and began sobbing.

The girls crowded forward and peered out after me. No one said anything.

Except Jill.

"I tried to stop her," she whispered to me, holding on tight to me as if her heart would break. "I tried to keep her from going out!"

"All right, Jill," I said soothingly.

"She wanted help—help in killing herself!" Jill said unbelievingly. "Can you imagine that?"

I did not say anything.

I thought of the girl who had been garroted. I thought of the girl who had drowned herself in the pond in back of the county home.

And now Lora Blake.

Yes. I could imagine it.

How had Lora Blake gotten back from the airport last night?

That was what I wanted to know.

Before the police came, I telephoned the airline that I had told Don to call.

Yes, they had received his call.

Yes, they had reserved a place for Miss Blake.

No, Miss Blake had never checked in at the airport.

No, Mrs. Hammond had never been seen at the airport either.

I hung up, staring at the phone and I could see everything beginning to spin about in front of me. Mrs. Hammond had never arrived at the airport ... *Never arrived* ...

PART TWO:

Ben Magruder

Chapter Seven

Lieutenant Michael Hardesty of the Coldwater Police Department was a very well-dressed man in his forties who had a short way with words and a brusque way with people.

We all stayed inside the building while the members of the Detective Department took photographs of poor Lora's body, of the building, and of the sidewalk. Then the ambulance came and drove off in the direction of Coldwater Hospital where the Medical Examiner would examine the body in the Morgue.

Pale-faced, we sat there in the lobby of the Hall, staring at one another and making occasional comments that told nothing but filled up the space between us with sound.

I could not look into my own heart—or my mind—for I knew that in some way I was responsible for Lora Blake's death. Had I not possessed the sense and the knowledge of a social worker to see that Lora Blake was a disturbed person, on the brink of a breakdown? Why had I not sensed her suicidal attitude?

Whenever I began to dissect my thoughts and reactions to her pleas, I immediately shut my mind away from analysis and stared moodily into the blank faces about me. Jill Towers had been weeping, but had finally regained her composure. Mrs. Grant sat white-faced and prim in a large chair, glancing at us one by one and grimacing with that evanescent smile of hers, which I am sure she turned on as automatically as you turn on a hot water faucet.

Mrs. Venefica, who had been discovered down the hall in Sandy Mason's room, would nervously pace the lobby, then seat herself and wriggle about in her chair until she had to get up again to pace up and down distractedly. Her eyes were full of horror and disbelief.

It was Lenore Ulrich whom I caught once watching me with questioning eyes. She was a blonde young girl, about nineteen, with light-blue eyes and a fair skin. Slender and willowy, she had an almost seraphic quality about her. Her eyes when I looked into them were quite outrageously probing, and I wondered for an instant why she was so forward as to be staring at me that way. Then she looked away, and I caught her only once after that considering me calculatingly.

I shivered, but then stiffened my back and continued the desultory vigil while Lieutenant Hardesty proceeded with his investigations in the room from which Lora Blake had jumped.

Finally, he appeared and closed the door behind him.

"Mrs. Grant, and residents of the Hall, I'll make this brief. You all know what happened to one of your colleagues, Lora Blake. On the face of it, Miss Blake died after a fall from a fourth floor window of the Hall. Now, because of the circumstances, I must make a preliminary investigation to determine if the death was an intentional action, an accident, or if it was caused advertantly or inadvertantly by someone else."

There was a hushed silence.

Lieutenant Hardesty glanced about him smoothly and went on.

"Just tell me what you know about Miss Blake, and I'll do this as quickly as possible. As I call your name, please come into the main office—" he glanced at Mrs. Grant—"if I may use your facilities, Mrs. Grant?"

"Of course, of course!" exclaimed Mrs. Grant, leaping up and smiling at the lieutenant. She raced out of the room to prepare her office.

And so we continued waiting, as first Mrs. Grant, and then Mrs. Venefica, and finally the girls began filing in one by one. There were eleven girls left when I was called.

As I went to Mrs. Grant's office I passed Lenore Ulrich just coming out of the doorway. She glanced at me briefly and then walked right on past me without a word.

I turned to watch her, puzzled at her rather strange behavior.

Steeling myself, I entered to face the lieutenant. I had decided that I would say as little as possible about Lora's strange visit to our home, unless directly asked. I had wished for time to telephone Don to ask his advice, but I had not been able to make the call in private.

Withholding evidence was a criminal offense, I knew, but actually all I would be doing was substantiating the theory that Lora Blake had taken her life because she was on the verge of a nervous breakdown.

Lieutenant Hardesty eyed me and smiled faintly. He was an extremely virile man, big in the shoulders, big in the legs, big in the chest. And his face was formed of hard planes and thick skin that had been closely-shaven some hours earlier. He wore an inexpensive suit very well, the folds of the garment fitting his frame admirably.

We went through the name and address bit easily enough. Finally, he leaned back in Mrs. Grant's chair and looked at me carefully.

"When was the last time you saw Lora Blake, Mrs. Hammond?"

"In Mrs. Venefica's room."

"You were there when she—when she went out the window," Hardesty mused. "Tell me, was there any reason for her to be struggling with Jill Towers?"

I shook my head. "I don't know, Lieutenant."

He nodded absently. "All right. Did Lora Blake and Jill Towers dislike each other?"

"No," I said immediately. "It seemed to me as if Jill was trying to keep Lora from jumping out the window."

"I see. In other words, you've formed the opinion already that Lora Blake *did* deliberately jump. Is that right?"

"Yes," I said slowly.

"You knew Lora fairly well?"

"As well as any of the girls." I was about to add more, but stopped, remembering my resolution just in time.

"How did she seem to you?"

I frowned. "What do you mean?"

"You're a trained social worker. I mean, what was her mental state? Was she calm?"

"On the contrary, she seemed distraught."

"Yes. Distraught about what, Mrs. Hammond?"

"I don't know," I said, hating to lie. "It seemed that she could not get along with the girls. She had led a sheltered life in Illinois. Coming to a place like this, with sophisticated people around her, she seemed lost."

Lieutenant Hardesty smiled faintly. "That's quite interesting."

"What is quite interesting?" I asked, suddenly disconcerted and almost a little afraid.

"You're the first one who has had that impression."

I suppose I turned pale. "Oh?"

"Yes. Most of them say Lora was depressed because her fiancé had been killed recently."

"Oh," I said. "Yes."

"But of course you're trained to see through façades like that, aren't you?"

I looked away. "I suppose so."

"What did you discuss with her last night?"

The breath absolutely squeezed out of my chest. I stared blankly at him for a long moment, my face turning cold.

"Last—night?"

"Yes. Lenore Ulrich said she saw Lora Blake get out of your car sometime about four o'clock in the early morning in front of the Hall. You let Lora into the Hall with your key, and then you drove away." He leaned forward, the force of his masculinity a tactile thing. "Isn't that the way it was, Mrs. Hammond?"

"She—she came to our house," I said finally, "in a cab."

Hardesty nodded, leaning back.

"She was distraught. My husband and I tried to calm her. The girl—I had talked to Lora before, and I found her quite upset, on the verge of some kind of mental breakdown. She was ingrown, inward-looking, inter-oriented. I'm saying it badly. She was a simple, somewhat immature girl. She was out of her element. The girls here frightened her. Her Bible teachings had been made fun of."

"What did you say?"

I repeated it. "The girls made fun of her beliefs. I'm only assuming, Lieutenant, but they must have teased her with some kind of Black Mass or witches' circle."

"Witches," muttered Hardesty contemptuously.

"But you see, Lora was a bit simpler than the rest of them. It frightened her. She believed that they were trying to steal her mind."

He snorted.

"I was not going to tell you any of this, because I know exactly how silly it sounds. And I do not for a moment believe that the magic circle had anything to do with her suicide. I think she simply had gotten out of her depth. Her fear of witchcraft was simply a symptom of her mental depression. That it affected her more than normal is only natural. She destroyed herself because she could not cope with life anymore, not simply because she was frightened of witches."

Hardesty cleared his throat. "I see. But you haven't told me why Lora Blake came out to your house."

I glanced away, ordering my thoughts. "Actually, she came out there to tell me she was afraid to live at the Hall. She wanted to stay with us. But Don—my husband—suggested that she go to California where she has an uncle. And so Lora agreed. Don and I had an argument about who would take her to the airport."

"Wait a moment. You were going to take Lora to the airport last night?"

"Well, early in the morning. Yes."

"What made you change your mind and bring her back here?" Hardesty's eyes were narrowed.

I swallowed hard. "Let me tell it my way, Lieutenant. My husband and I argued, and when Don went in to dress, I put on a raincoat over my robe, and got the car out. We were out of the driveway before Don saw us. I drove off, up to the Merritt Parkway, and to New York." My voice faltered.

"Did Lora change her mind then?" Hardesty asked.

I looked away again. "Actually, Lieutenant, I don't know *what* happened."

His face tightened, the eyes alert and intent. "You don't know?"

I blinked my eyes, almost tearfully. "I paid the first toll, Lieutenant, and then—I swear to you—I cannot remember what happened after that until I came to and found myself in the house again!"

There was a long silence.

Finally, Lieutenant Hardesty scribbled words on a pad in front of him, and then lifted his face once again to me.

"You don't remember delivering Lora Blake to the front door of the Hall, opening the door for her with your key, and then driving off?"

I shook my head, unable to speak in the panic that was welling up within me.

"I see." The breath expelled from his chest. He leaned back and contemplated me. His voice was lazy, flat, and suddenly impertinent. "We have a situation in which a trained social worker, sensing a girl's despondency, tries to help her by escaping from an intolerable situation. She drives her off in a car, ostensibly headed for escape, but in actuality headed right back to the Hall where the girl cannot cope, and *lets her in*. Mrs. Hammond, is that the story you want me to believe?"

"It's the truth," I whispered.

He heaved his shoulders in a kind of bear shrug. "It sounds mighty strange to me, Mrs. Hammond."

Speechless, I nodded.

"But it has the ring of truth," he said, looking down at his notes. "And it meshes with everything else that has been said already. Although there has been no mention of witchcraft from anyone else. I believe the girl might have been stretching the truth there a little, in order to involve you in her own problem. She knew you were a trained psychologist."

"Yes," I said with a sigh.

"All right. Let's move on to Lora's death. Your story is that you came to Mrs. Venefica's room when you heard the screams, and saw Lora Blake struggling with Jill Towers, who was ostensibly trying to prevent her from going out the window. Right?"

"Yes sir."

"But you couldn't help her any more than Jill Towers could, and she went out."

"Yes sir."

He studied his notes. "There's one thing I don't like the looks of, Mrs. Hammond."

"Sir?"

"That blackout of yours. This memory lapse. I believe you, actually. But I mention this for a good reason. If you have suffered from a blackout of that nature, I would strongly suggest that you see a doctor. Now, *you* know that as well as I do, Mrs. Hammond. I'm surprised you haven't made any effort to analyze yourself."

I struggled weakly with my embarrassment. "I have already decided to undergo analysis, Lieutenant. With Dr. Strachey."

His eyes came up and held mine a moment. "I see. A good man, Mrs. Hammond. A very good man."

"Is—is that all?"

"That's all," Hardesty said, and looked at the papers in front of him. "Will you send in June Moore?"

"Yes sir," I said, and escaped.

Dr. Leland Strachey lived in one of the few remaining old-fashioned, Colonial structures left in Coldwater. It was a white, clapboard house with early New England gables in a mansard roof. Shutters bordered every window of the house. There was a long verandah-type front porch, with lawn furniture set out at random intervals.

An elderly woman showed me in and took me into an old, paneled parlor where the overstuffed furniture had antimacassars draped over the tops. Reproductions of early American scenes hung on the walls in inexpensive frames. There was a Tiffany lamp hanging over a small table in the corner of the room. Potted plants grew on ornate metal stands. An oriental rug had been placed in the middle of the oaken floor. The room cried of clutter, but it was officially Victorian clutter, and acceptably stylish in its own way.

"Is the doctor expecting you?" the woman asked. She resembled an old rooster, with wattles where her throat should be.

"Yes ma'am," I said. "I called him this morning and he agreed to see me."

She nodded and left the room.

I stared around me and shifted in the chair. Within minutes she came back, beckoned, and led me into a room off the parlor which had been set up as an informal office.

There was a desk in one corner of the room, a stiff-backed, red chair facing it, and a long old-fashioned divan next to a window. Another stiff-backed chair stood just behind the couch, between it and the window.

When I entered, the room was deserted. The woman left and I looked around at the same faded reproductions on the walls, the same type of oriental rug on the floor, and the divan, chairs, and desk placed in the corners of the room.

The far door opened and a tall, well-dressed, middle-aged man with gray-streaked hair strode in. He was fingering a small blond-wood pipe in his fingers, smiling behind his large, steel-rimmed, mod glasses. He waved his free hand at me to relax.

"Mrs. Hammond, isn't it?" he asked as he got into the chair behind the desk. "Won't you sit down, please?" He indicated the stiff-backed chair facing him.

I got up and settled into it uncomfortably.

"Dr. Kingsley mentioned you, of course," he said

with a quick smile on his long, thin face. "He said you were experiencing a recurring dream." Dr. Strachey glanced up, his liquid, green eyes large behind the lenses of his steel-rimmed glasses. "Is that true?"

"Yes," I said.

"Well, then, I suppose there is something we can do to help." He paused, fingered his pipe, put it in his mouth carefully, and puffed on it. Without removing the pipe, but shifting it to the corner of his mouth where his side teeth gripped the stem, he spoke to me with a twisted kind of diction.

"Now then, how is your sex life, Mrs. Hammond?"

I suppose I flushed. "Fine, Dr. Strachey."

Strachey looked amused. "Now, what kind of word is 'fine', Mrs. Hammond?" He smirked. "It's like terrible. Nobody wants to use the word 'terrible', because, you see, it's a *terrible* word!" He chuckled. "And 'fine' is much the same. A 'fine' word—may be *too fine*. You see?"

I nodded. "I guess so."

"And your sex life is—adequate?" Dr. Strachey intoned, puffing at his pipe.

"I am in love with my husband, Dr. Strachey," I said with some heat. "Is that what you are asking me?"

"Oh, heavens no," he replied. "Every wife is in love with her husband. What I asked you specifically was: How is your sex life?"

"Excellent!"

Dr. Strachey considered. "Well, that's better than *fine,* anyway."

"Now. Perhaps you should ask my husband. You know?" I was annoyed.

The green, liquid eyes probed mine. Smoke rose between us. "My, you are touchy about sex, aren't you? But that's fine, really fine! I had hoped for some reaction. We know now that there *is* some problem there. Don't we?"

"I don't. Perhaps you do. *You* is not not *we*."

Dr. Strachey smiled and gurgled. "I like that. I like that."

"Dr. Strachey. We seem to be getting nowhere," I

said. "I was cautioned again today that I should see a psychiatrist. And that was because I could not remember something that happened last night."

Dr. Strachey stopped smiling. "Indeed?"

"Yes, Dr. Strachey."

"A blackout?"

I nodded.

"Amnesia?" He leaned forward, puffing furiously. "A recurring dream. And now amnesia. Ah yes. Yes. Dr. Kingsley did not mention the blackout."

"It had not occurred when we spoke."

"I see. Then this is recent."

"As recent as twenty-four hours ago," I snapped. "Can we get on with it?"

Dr. Strachey stood up, puffed on his pipe, and turned to me. "Well, now, it isn't all that easy, you know. It takes time. Time and a great deal of probing." He smiled. "I do have to get the *facts* of your life straight before we begin. Now, shall we do so?"

I slumped in the chair, as much as I *could* slump in a straight-backed chair.

"Now then," he said, and took out a pad of yellow, lined paper from his middle drawer and smoothed it out in front of him. "Shall we begin?"

I nodded.

And he began asking me questions about my life; where I was born; when; when I was married; all the facts.

But nothing else.

An hour later we were through.

"Well," he said, beaming at me. "I think that we are now able to start."

"Good," I said.

"We'll set up your first appointment next week. Say Monday? And Wednesday? And Friday?"

I said, "Yes." It was the first time I realized that he would not be asking me any more questions for now. Slightly disappointed, but at the same time somewhat relieved, I shook hands with him and walked out into the sunlight.

Chapter Eight

Don was aghast, of course, when I told him the news. He simply could not believe it.

"She jumped out the window of the Hall?" he repeated incredulously. "But I thought she had flown by jet plane to California!"

I turned to him, pleadingly.

But he was paying attention to driving and did not see my guilty look.

"How did she get back to the Hall?"

I tried to think of some sensible answer.

"Well, I suppose for some reason she went back. After pretending to get on board that plane, she took a cab to the Hall in Coldwater."

I turned from Don, staring straight ahead, unable to control the elation that surged within me. I had not been forced to lie at all; nor had I been forced to tell the truth, which, I felt, would have been the most difficult thing of all.

"Well," said Don, thinking about it as we continued up along the river toward the house. "She struck me as being pretty much a psychotic, I guess you'd call it. Right?"

"Yes," I said feebly.

"But it's too bad she wasn't under a doctor's care instead of being let loose in that crazy Hall." He turned to me briefly. "I don't like that place, Aimee, and I want you to leave it."

"Don, we've been through this before, and I don't want to have to go through it again tonight. I'm tired.

There were police officers there, and everything. It was a very long day. And Dr. Strachey was rather overbearing, too."

Don's face lighted up. "You saw Strachey?"

"Yes," I said with a smile. "I took your advice."

That mollified him. "I'm sure you won't regret it, Aimee," he said enthusiastically. "I'm surprised you didn't go to him right away when that stupid dream started."

"I was timid," I admitted.

"Now I'm sure you'll be all right! It's probably just something in your susubsconscious."

"You sound like a psychiatrist yourself," I teased him.

"You, of all people, should have known when you needed a doctor!" he chided me.

"I slipped up," I said.

Don considered. "Those foolish games," he mused. "I think they're harmless, of course, but do you think there's really anything in them? I mean, enough to make that poor girl jump to her death?"

"What foolish games?" I repeated innocently, although I knew exactly what he meant.

"Those 'witches' games. The magic circle. The chanting. That kind of thing."

I shook my head. "Simply something to pass the time. Do you see anything wrong in yoga exercises? Or in kung fu lessons? Of course not. Witchcraft is the same thing, really. Just a harmless fad."

Don frowned. "I hardly think a Black Mass is as innocent as a lesson in kung fu," Don said slowly. "But perhaps it isn't anything to get uptight about."

"Of course not," I said airily.

We were turning into the driveway. "I'd still like you to quit your job and get something else, Aimee," he said as he brought the car to a stop. He turned to me. "I don't want to—to lose you," he said with a suddenly, choked voice.

The blackout. The dream. The terrible feeling of being *managed*. I turned away from him hastily.

"You won't!" I said with as much determination as I could. "You won't!"

I hoped, anyway. *I hoped*.

We were lolling over our coffee when the telephone rang. I frowned at Don and he lifted an eyebrow. Who could be calling us at this inconvenient hour? We did not have that many friends in Coldwater.

I lifted the handset. "Hello?"

And it was a woman with a flat, masculine voice, informing me that Ben Magruder had had a heart attack that afternoon and that he was now resting at his own home with a nurse—the telephone caller—in attendance. And Ben would like to see us. His doctor had permitted him to have guests and we could come over now if we liked.

I hung up, my face obviously pale.

"What is it?" Don asked quickly, rising and standing next to me.

"Ben. He's—he's had a heart attack!" I stared up at Don, and I could barely see him through the tears in my eyes. I remembered how sickly Ben had looked when I had seen him for the first time after moving to Coldwater. And now . . .

"How is he?" Don asked quickly.

"There's a nurse there. He wants us to come over."

Don's face cleared. "Then he's probably all right. His doctor wouldn't allow it if he wasn't on the mend. Let's go, Aimee!"

"Yes," I said, still tearful, but blowing my nose with a handkerchief as I put the dishes away in the washer and started it up.

We found Ben in his little cottage in the Ridges propped up in his bed reading a book. He looked, if anything, better than the last time I had seen him. The nurse, a battleship-shaped woman with steel-gray eyes and an enormous, unshapely bosom, stood brooding at us and at Ben until Ben waved her away.

"Please, Mrs. Bensonhurst. I'll let you know if I need anything."

"Yes, Mr. Magruder," she said, glanced icily at the two of us as she sailed out of the room.

Ben laid down his book and patted the bed at his side. "Here, Aimee." He pointed to the chair next to the bed. "Don. Sit."

We did so.

Ben scratched his beard and took off his glasses for just a moment, wiped them with the edge of the bed sheet, and put them back on again, looking at me first and then at Don.

"Let's make a pact. We won't talk about it. I had a heart attack. I've recovered. I'm on the mend. Dr. Gillespie says I'll be all right, with luck. And that's all there is to it."

"We're glad you're looking so well," Don mumbled.

"Right, Ben!" I said, grasping his hand and squeezing it.

Ben flushed. "A pretty young girl might upset Gillespie's calculations," he said with a wink. "Look. This is serious. Don't try to get me off the track. I've been doing a lot of research on that—" his eyes moved to me— "that *Hall* where you work."

Don snorted. "You haven't heard the latest!"

"The latest?"

I stiffened. "Don! Later!"

Don stared at me, about to argue, then thought better of it and remained silent.

Ben glanced from him to me and then back to Don. "Okay. Then tell me later. But now I want to talk about that Resident Hall!"

"Right," I said weakly.

"I've been researching a lot of things I made notes on while I was there at that October Fest you had."

"Not October Fest. October Social," I said, correcting him with a smile.

"No," Ben said, shaking his head emphatically. "October fest. Don't you understand the significance of October?"

I frowned. "What about October?"

"October was called 'Winterfallyn,' by the Anglo-

84

Saxons because Winter was supposed to begin at the end of October," Ben said seriously.

I laughed. "What has that to do—"

Ben held up a hand. "The Druids lit bonfires on the last night of October in the belief that of all nights in the year this was the one during which ghosts and witches were most likely to wander abroad. They lit the fires in honor of the Sun-god in thanksgiving for the harvest. And they believed that on this evening, Saman, the lord of death, called together the wicked souls that within the past twelve months had been condemned to inhabit the bodies of animals. In some parts of Ireland, even now, the end of October is still called Oidhche Shamhna, the 'Vigil of Saman.' "

"But you're simply describing Halloween," I scoffed. "And we had our Social before Halloween!"

"But the October Social symbolized Hallows, or Samhain, as it is called in certain quarters," Ben said heavily. "And I've been doing more work on the notes I took that night."

"Notes?" Don asked politely.

"Yes. In addition to the pentacle—"

"What pentacle?" Don asked.

I glanced at Ben Magruder in alarm. Why had he suddenly brought up the pentacle again? We had gone all through that before, and had decided that it was simply part of the game the girls on the fourth floor were playing with old Mrs. Venefica to keep her happy.

"The pentacle drawn under the doormat at the Hall," Ben said softly.

"That's fine," Don said sarcastically. "You've answered my question, but I still don't know a pentacle from a panicle."

"A pentacle is a sacred diagram, a drawing of a five-pointed star. It's used by witches in incantations, to protect them from other witches."

Don was staring at Ben Magruder as if Ben had two heads. I almost had to smother a laugh.

"Witches? It's a hex mark?"

"No. The opposite of a hex mark, Don. It's a protective device."

"But, Ben—witches?" Don's brow rose high in disdain.

"That's why I want to talk to you and Aimee."

"Oh." Don looked at me and leaned back in his chair.

"All right," said Ben. "There's the pentacle. We already discussed that. Did you find it?"

"I found it," I admitted.

Ben picked up a sheet of paper that he was using as a book-mark in the volume he had been reading. "Two. Here's another thing I didn't tell you about, because I simply didn't know whether or not the presence of the horns was a coincidence or not."

"Horns?" Don repeated, incredulously.

"Ram's horns," Ben said. "They're hanging on the doorway of one of the rooms on the fourth floor. I happened to notice them as I passed by. The door was open and—"

"What about ram's horns?"

"Well, again they're used in witchcraft. 'Old Cornus' is another name for the Devil. Satan has cloven feet as you know. So does the ram. Ram's horns are symbols of the devil."

Don nodded. "Go on." His voice sounded weak.

"Well, then, three. There is a clay pot of *verbens hortensis* in Mrs. Venefica's room."

"*Verbens hortensis?*" I asked.

"It's known as verbana—garden verbena—to most people. But in Europe it's known as 'vervain,' and it is the most potent of all herbs used in counter-sorcery. It has been called 'enchanter's herb' for that very reason."

Don said nothing.

"But Ben," I said. "That could simply be the old lady's idea of something to grow."

Ben held up his hand again. "Four. In the small garden plot outside the building, there's another plant closely associated through the centuries with witchcraft. *Hypericum androsaeum.* Also known as Tutsan St. John's-wort. It's a wine-colored, juicy fruit, which has curative properties well known to sorcerers."

There was silence.

"Well," Ben said, looking from Don to me, "what do you think about that?"

"I think it's all a coincidence," I said spiritedly, "and I'm not going to let you try to frighten me."

"I never heard about that pentacle before," Don said, looking a moment at me in silent reproof. "Why didn't you tell me, Aimee?"

"Don. Ben and I often talk about things that I don't pass on to you. I thought the finding of the pentacle was very entertaining, but I thought you would laugh at it if you heard about it. That's the reason I didn't tell you."

Don nodded. "I'll accept that for now." He frowned. "That's four different things, isn't it, Ben? You've really gone to a lot of work."

Ben Magruder ran his hands through his unruly hair. "I was worried from the moment I entered the Hall. It's got a very bad history. And there's something definitely *wrong* there."

Don rubbed his chin. "Witchcraft, eh?"

"Witchcraft," said Ben. "I'll be frank with you, Don. I don't like it one bit."

"Do you *believe* in witchcraft?" Don asked flatly, looking directly in Ben Magruder's eyes.

"I believe in the *results* of witchcraft," Ben shot back.

"That means you do believe that witchcraft can be practiced!" Don said.

"I mean that there are things that cannot be explained by science."

"Witchcraft being one of them?" Don asked.

"Right."

"Ben," I said. "Please. Don't let's go into this any more. We're all adult, mature, people. We all know that this is strictly nonsense. We know there isn't anything *to* witchcraft!"

"*Something* happened in Salem," Ben retorted. "What was that but witchcraft, Aimee?"

My heart was in my throat. I felt dizzy. I shook myself and steadied down. "That was mass hysteria," I said stoutly. "I've read about those trials. It was mass hypnosis—self-deception—in troubled political times. It can all be explained scientifically."

Ben chuckled. "Oh, certainly. I've read the Freudian interpretation. A group of spoiled, teen-aged girls with nothing to do, playing games with an entire community."

"Well?" I challenged him.

"There was certainly more to it than that, Aimee. People believed in witchcraft in those days. And because they believed, there *was* witchcraft. Those girls were not name-callers and shouters just for a lark. Have you examined the records? They were, literally, twisted into inhuman shapes by convulsions. Their tongues were extended from their mouths and their arms and legs were crossed so tightly they could not be uncrossed without fear of breaking their bones!"

I glanced at Don, who was staring at Ben in fascination.

"No, Aimee," Ben grumbled. "It was not just a simple exercise in mass deception. There was *something else* at work there. Those girls practiced witchcraft and because they believed in witchcraft they were subjected to real physical tortures. In a society that believes in witchcraft, it works. If you believe in witchcraft and you find that someone has been holding your image in the form of a doll over a flame or muttering charms over your nail-parings, you will probably become extremely sick. Your symptoms will be psychosomatic rather than organic. But that does not mean the symptoms are any less terrible. And they will seem to be the result of demonic power rather than simple sickness. And that was the way it was in New England in 1692!"

"I see what you mean," Don broke in, much to my annoyance. "You're saying that everyone becomes swept up in the belief that the devil is after them, and the devil does *then* exist!"

Ben nodded. "Besides, the Salem witch trials were not the first in New England. In 1654 a woman named Mrs. Anne Hibbins was hanged for a witch. Later, in 1662, a certain Anne Cole had fits, in which she spoke in strange voices not her own. She confessed to being a witch, and was let off as a hysteric. Rebecca Greensmith was hanged in 1663. And in 1688 an Irish woman named Glover actually confessed to believing in Satan rather than God, and her spells affected all four girls in the John Goodwin family. So the stage was set for 1692 for the Salem business. It was not any special isolated instance."

"And you don't think those people were psychotic?" I asked scornfully.

"Certainly they were psychotic, to use our current phrase. But psychotic or not, they were motivated to their state of madness by witchcraft or the belief in witchcraft—and not by anything else. If the social situation is such that witchcraft can flourish, it will." Ben paused and stared at me intently. "Given the right circumstances, I think even you could be made to believe in witchcraft, Aimee!"

"Not me!" I laughed.

Don shook his head. "She's too level-headed, Ben. I'm afraid you said the wrong thing there."

Ben smiled faintly. "Once witchcraft or the fear of it is abroad, *everyone* can find witches to burn!"

Don smiled. "I guess that's been proven time and time again!"

Ben turned to me. "Aimee, what about the girl who was garroted? And the girl who jumped out of the window of the rest home?"

Don also turned to me. "Well?"

I shook my head. "My mind isn't changed. *They* were each psychotic, disturbed girls. One was murdered. Who knows who did it? The other went out of her head and committed suicide."

"But Aimee," Ben interrupted. "Don't you realize that garroting is a most familiar way to dispose of a witch? In Scotland, for example, a confessed or discovered witch was garroted first, then burned at the stake. Don't you see why I've been worried ever since hearing about Willa Gayle?"

"Willa Gayle?" I repeated.

"That was her name," said Ben, his face turning the slightest bit red. "Yes, I've been looking up the records! She was born in New York and came to live here at the Hall just before she was found murdered. Why was she garroted? You see, it *does* bring up natural questions. And the name . . ."

"What name?" Don asked brusquely.

"Her name." Ben frowned. "Never mind. It's just a theory. I haven't been able to prove a thing."

"What was the second girl's name?"

"The one who drowned herself in the pond? Her name was Ellen Putnam." Ben smiled. "You see, I have been doing a great deal of homework."

"The devil's work!" I scoffed.

His eyes were wide. "Aimee," he chided me. But I could see that behind the glint of humor his expression was serious.

Don cleared his throat. "Willa Gayle. Ellen Putnam. And that brings us up to Lora Blake."

Ben Magruder looked up. "Who's Lora Blake?"

"A girl at the Hall," I said, hesitantly. "At least—"

"She died last night, Ben," snapped Don, angry at me for not telling him outright. "She jumped out of a window at the Hall and killed herself."

Ben's face paled and I thought he might sink back unconscious in his bed. "Last night?"

I nodded stubbornly. "Believe me, Ben, she was psychotic. There was every reason to believe, from her past history, that she might take her own life. It had nothing—"

"What *time*?" Ben asked in a hoarse voice.

I glanced at Don, but he was not looking at me. "About—about four o'clock this afternoon."

Ben Magruder closed his eyes and turned his head away from us. "My God," he whispered.

"What *is* it?" Don asked anxiously.

Ben's eyes came open and fixed on me. "At four o'clock I was in my study, working on those notes. And, suddenly, I was not in my room at all, but *falling through the air*! And when I came to—" Ben Magruder looked up at the ceiling, his face grimacing in remembered pain—"I was in the middle of a heart seizure. It was as if someone had stuck some kind of *blade* in my chest—a burning—"

Don's eyes were wide. "Say that again!"

"A pain in my chest, as if someone had stuck a knife in it!"

Don turned to me. "Tell Ben how Lora Blake died."

"She—*fell*—from the top floor of the Hall—from Mrs. Venefica's room—and she fell onto the spikes in the fence in front of the garden plot."

Ben Magruder blinked. "The knife in my chest!"

Don and I stared.

"But why—?" Ben Magruder closed his eyes. "Aimee, I was thinking of you when I was doing that work for you. I'm frightened for you. Do you hear me? Frightened!"

"But, Ben, it's all a coincidence! Lora Blake came running to us last night, asking for sanctuary against evil forces trying to steal her brain! She was a hopeless psychotic, Ben! Believe me, there was nothing there to indicate a practice in witchcraft."

Don frowned. "Wait. She did say she was indulging in rites with Mrs. Venefica."

"That's the woman with the vervain, the one who brews tea," said Ben. "A common witch activity."

"But why?" I asked.

"Why what?" Ben responded.

"Why would *she* want to kill Lora Blake?"

"She didn't want to," said Ben Magruder softly.

"But the girl jumped!" Don said equably.

Ben turned to me. "Possession, my dear." And he smiled a kind of smirk.

"Possession?" I asked.

"Yes. The Salem girls. Don't you remember? Each was possessed by the spirit of the Devil!"

"That's what they *said*," I countered.

"Nevertheless, that would certainly be a motive to entice the girl into a witch's circle."

"Why?"

"To make her susceptible to suggestion, to train the girl's spirit to leave her body, and then for the witch *to enter the body*!"

Don was staring at Ben as if he were demented. "Are you serious?"

"Never more serious," said Ben in a low voice. "Mrs. Venefica, from what I saw of her, is a sick, old, dying woman. The witch's spirit does not die, it cannot go to heaven, or hell. It is trapped forever in limbo. And where better to go than from a dying old body like Mrs. Venefica's into the young, untried body of a girl like Lora Blake?"

Don was staring at me.

"Yes," I said almost as if I doubted my own sanity. "She *did* tell us that 'someone' was trying to steal her brain. She meant spirit. She meant someone was trying to steal into her body and *become* her!" I was aghast.

Don's eyes widened. "Of course!"

Ben Magruder cleared his throat. "I realize how strange this sounds, but it is not quite so far-fetched as you might think. All the recorded histories of possession have involved much the same thing. In several cases, the invading spirit was simply the Devil. But in other cases, certain friends or acquaintances of the victim tried to enter the body, to bedevil it, if you will, or to force it to do strange things. Who knows whether or not hundreds of other bodies might have been entered by other spirits quietly so that no one ever knew, but simply said, 'Old John isn't himself anymore.' Or 'Old Mary has changed.' You've heard that many times?"

Don slowly turned to face me. "Aimee. That's what your dream is, of course."

"Dream?" I repeated. My mind had been somewhere else.

"The burning dream," said Ben Magruder. "That's what I wanted to talk to you about next. It's a favorite method of torment—burning. The idea is to make the victim so uncomfortable that he wills himself to escape from the heat and the pain, and the body becomes an empty hull."

"Aimee!" cried Don, his face that of a stranger. "You must leave that place!"

"I absolutely order it!" said Ben Magruder, his eyes holding mine.

"I won't do it!" I snapped right back. "You're talking a lot of nonsense!"

"Aimee, dearest," Ben Magruder said, "you must not take the chance! You must get out of that Hall at once! You're the obvious victim, even if you don't believe Lora Blake was. You come from Salem, you have a well-known possessed girl's name, and you are dreaming strange dreams. Aimee, if you go back there, you're in danger of your life! Believe me!"

Don came up and lifted me to my feet, his strong hands around my wrists. "Aimee, I've been kidding before, but this time I think Ben Magruder is right! Sure, we know witchcraft is a joke. And we don't really know what killed Lora Blake. But you've been acting strangely, and that weird dream is certainly not like you. I think there's something evil at that place that's trying to possess you. Just like Ben said!"

I shook off his hands. "No!" I was angry. "I'm not some kind of child you can order around! Don, I'm your wife! We pledged ourselves to each other as husband and wife. We share each other's aims and aspirations. If I quit my job now because I was afraid of some idiotic thing like possession, I could never face myself again!"

"But, Aimee," Don said.

"Aimee, you're making a mistake!" intoned Ben Magruder.

I turned to look down at Ben Magruder. Poor Ben! The heart attack had left its mark on him. He had been haggard and pale from tension, from anxiety, from some kind of debilitating weakness the last time we had seen him. But now he had aged ten years. He was a pitiful man. And pitiful, old men always envy those who are strong and young.

He envied me. He envied me my job at the Hall. Somehow he wanted me to fail. And because he knew my one weakness—the fact that I was ashamed for having come from Salem, where the witches were hanged —he was trying to pull me down to his level.

That was what motivated him in this mad desire to make me stop work.

I smiled at him gently.

"Oh, Ben," I said. "I'm not making a mistake. I'm going back to work tomorrow. And you'll be feeling better yourself!" I walked to the door with Don. "Now have some rest and get cured, Ben. You'll want to know what Dr. Strachey finds out about my psyche, won't you?"

He would not wave at me. He simply stared at me with hollow eyes. He was frightened. For a split second I too was frightened. But I resolutely turned away, took Don't arm, and went out through the doorway into the other room where we bid Mrs. Bensonhurst goodnight.

"Aimee!" cried Ben from the bedroom.

I went back in.

He held out a door key. "Take this. Mrs. Bensonhurst is only on during the evening. I may not be able to get up to let you in. Take it. And keep in touch, Aimee. I'm frightened for you."

Chapter Nine

For several days after the death of Lora Blake Mrs. Venefica was very sick. She kept to her bed at the rear of her little office on the fourth floor, with only Jill Towers bringing food in to her.

I went in to see her several times, the first time during the afternoon of the next day.

"Oh, Mrs. Hammond," she trilled at me from her prone position, "how nice of you to come visit me."

"I'm sorry you're not feeling well," I said, and seated myself next to her bed.

She looked ghastly. Without the slightest bit of makeup, and with her hair in knots and tangles about her parchment-white skull, she looked more dead than alive. Only the black, burning coals of her eyes were in any sense the same as ever.

"It's all the excitement and the horror of that poor girl's death," sighed Mrs. Venefica. "I can't help but think myself responsible for her going out the window that way."

"Why do you feel responsible, Mrs. Venefica?" I asked, my curiosity immediately aroused. I remembered what Ben Magruder had said about the special herbs she grew in the pots around her desk.

"It's because she chose my office," Mrs. Venefica said immediately. "Don't you see?"

"Where were you when she jumped?" I asked quietly.

She blinked and turned away momentarily. Then she eyed me brightly once again. "I was tired, you see. I simply haven't been myself lately. And I was lying down in one of the girl's rooms. I don't even remember which one." Her eyes went vague, but then brightened. "And I heard a terrible commotion, and when I came to myself and struggled down the hall, it was all over." She closed her eyes and shook her head sadly.

"What do you know about Lora Blake, Mrs. Venefica?" I asked.

"Whatever do you mean?"

"Exactly what I say. Did you think she was troubled? Did you think she might have been on the verge of taking her own life?"

"Never!" Mrs. Venefica maintained stoutly. "Never! I simply considered her as one more of my girls and—"

"—and you taught her the rites!" I ventured.

There was a dead silence.

"Rites?" she repeated carefully.

"The rituals. The magic circle. The incantations."

Mrs. Venefica chuckled brightly. "Children's play, Mrs. Hammond. Children's play. Yes. She joined in with us in our games."

"Decidedly strange games, Mrs. Venefica," I said softly. "Decidedly strange."

"There is a growing interest in the occult and in the cult of witchcraft, Mrs. Hammond," Mrs. Venefica said, smiling that rather toothless-crone smile of hers. "But nothing to worry your poor head about, child. It was simply play."

"Something disturbed her, Mrs. Venefica. She took her own life because she felt her mind was being possessed—or as she put it, 'stolen away.'"

Mrs. Venefica frowned. "Oh, dear," she said. "Well, of course, that is the way one feels sometimes. I had no idea that she was taking it so seriously. Really, it was only fun and games."

"Then you *were* practicing witchcraft, Mrs. Venefica?" I asked in a voice so mild I was surprised it was my own.

"Merely following the words in the book, you know," she said with a modest smile. "We never really *did* anything."

"But you sang the songs. You repeated the words."

"Oh, yes!" She giggled. "It's sport, you know!"

"Has Lieutenant Hardesty spoken to you yet, Mrs. Venefica?"

"Yes," she said.

"What did you tell him?"

"I told him that Lora Blake was a nice girl and that she was a very dear friend of mine."

"And—about the witchcraft?"

Mrs. Venefica frowned. "But my dear of course I said nothing about that, because he didn't ask, now, did he? And besides, policemen are busy people. They do not like to hear about fun and games, do they, Mrs. Hammond?"

I said, "No more games, Mrs. Venefica. Do you understand me?"

Mrs. Venefica's face fell. "Well, I can understand you, yes. But I don't think they should cause any trouble. You can't just ignore interest in the occult, you know."

"But we can cease playing such games here at the

Hall, Mrs. Venefica," I said sternly. "If you persist, I'm afraid I'll have to speak to Mrs. Grant."

Mrs. Venefica's face showed real fear. "Oh, please don't do that, Mrs. Hammond. Please, don't!" Terror brightened the dark eyes. "Do you think she suspects, Mrs. Hammond?"

I shook my head. "I'm the only one who really knows, Mrs. Venefica. Let's leave it that way. Shall we? But no more of it, or I will tell Mrs. Grant and the Board of Directors."

"Oh, then I promise! I promise!" Her eyes were darting back and forth like trapped little animals.

"This has all been a most unfortunate affair," I said. "A girl has died. Now I want no more of it. Do you understand?"

"Oh, yes, Mrs. Hammond!"

"When did it all start?" I asked finally, because it had just occurred to me that perhaps Mrs. Venefica had something to do with the death by garroting and the earlier death by suicide.

"Oh, several months ago. It was just a lark, Mrs. Hammond."

I nodded. "All right, then." I reached over and took Mrs. Venefica's hand. It was ice cold. "I hope you'll be feeling better soon," I told her.

"Thank you," she said brightly.

Stupid woman! I thought. To a young, impressionable girl like Lora Blake, all that dabbling in the occult would make a deep impression on her simple mind. And Lora had been unable to balance up the excitement with common sense and experience. Somehow she had begun to believe she was possessed, and she had killed herself out of fear of the Devil.

Or perhaps her dip into the occult had simply upset her already unbalanced mind and caused her to destroy herself.

I briefly considered revealing the "magic circle" and the "incantations" to Lieutenant Hardesty, and then I decided that Mrs. Venefica was right: he simply would not believe it.

We had experienced enough trouble at the Hall. It was time to close the curtain on a very tragic event. And there was no reason to upset Mrs. Grant with a report of my confrontation with Mrs. Venefica. She was a hard-working woman, and it would upset her to know that she had not really been on top of her job. I decided to take the responsibility for the rituals myself.

I would tell no one. But I would watch Mrs. Venefica and the girls to be sure there was no repetition of the rites. Ben Magruder had stressed the fact that you did not need to believe in witchcraft to have it operate—if someone else believed. I concluded that just such a thing had happened here. Perhaps no one of the thirteen people involved had believed: but things had happened.

No more. Yet I must keep my eyes on the girls as well as Mrs. Venefica.

My visit to Dr. Strachey came almost as a relief after a tense and depressing day at the Hall.

He was cheerful and ebullient as ever.

"Today we begin with preliminaries," he said, chuckling somewhat absent-mindedly as he took his place in the chair behind the couch.

I reclined, looking at the ceiling with half-closed eyes.

"Yes sir," I said.

"As you know, my name is Dr. Strachey. Dr. Lyle Strachey. If you wish, you could call me Lyle, although I do not recommend it during this first session."

I smiled.

"Later, perhaps, yes. But I shall call you Aimee from the first."

"Yes, sir," I said.

"I like the name Aimee. It means 'loved,' you know."

"I did not know," I admitted.

"Then you never took French?"

"Never. I took English and Latin."

"I see. Aimee means 'loved'."

"You said that."

"Are you uncomfortable, or nervous?" he asked me solicitously as he leaned over me.

"Not at all, Dr. Strachey."

"But I note an agitation in your manner, a fluttering of the eyelids as if in great distress. Why?"

"I am not at all in distress!" I snapped.

"I see," he said, leaning back so I could not see him. He wrote in his notebook. I wondered what he was writing. "Aimee means loved." What a ridiculous thing!

"Why do you consider yourself unloved, Aimee?" he asked suddenly after a pause.

"I beg your pardon?"

"You're blocking out an answer, Aimee. Please answer immediately, with the first words you think of. The whole procedure here is to find out what you think and feel *spontaneously*. You see?"

"Yes, of course, I see," I said irritably.

"Why do you consider yourself—"

"I do not consider myself unloved!" I cried out.

"You protest too much," Dr. Strachey said. "I quote Will Shakespeare, of course. But he was one of the greatest psychologists of all time. You are overstressing your objections to the implications contained in my question."

"I am *not*!"

"Where were you born, Aimee?"

"In Massachusetts," I said immediately.

"Interesting," he sighed.

"What is interesting?" I asked. How irritating the man had become!

"When I ask a person where he lives, he says, 'London, England,' or 'Los Angeles, California,' or just 'Denver.'" Dr. Strachey paused. "Never—'Massachusetts.'"

"Nevertheless I *was* born in Massachusetts!" I snapped.

"Young lady—where in Massachusetts?"

"Salem."

"Salem!" He had known that, of course, from his earlier data collected at the first meeting. But I was too angry at him to question him as to why he played surprised. He already knew!

"Is there something about Salem that you do not like?"

"Nothing at all," I said.

"You have great hostility toward Salem," Dr. Strachey contradicted me. "First, you would not say the name of the place. And now you answer a question with a sweeping generality. If you had said, 'No,' or 'I don't think so,' I would have accepted that as the truth. But 'nothing at all' means, 'I do not like something about Salem.' "

I said nothing.

"Well, Aimee? What is it you do not like about Salem?"

"I don't know," I said, mocking him.

"I can't accept that answer now," he said smoothly. "Is it the fact that people make fun of you when you mention Salem? Because of the witches?"

Witches again!

"Aimee?"

I realized I had not answered him. And at the moment I could not remember where my mind had wandered after thinking about witches.

"I'm sorry. I am not too alert today."

"You're very alert. Now answer me. Is it because of the witches?"

"No. It is because people do make fun of me when I mention Salem."

"Ah! What was your father's name, Aimee?"

"William."

"I see. And—" pause "—his last name?"

"Parris," I said reluctantly.

"I see. Parris. And your name was Aimee Parris before your marriage to Don Hammond."

"A great big 'A' for effort!" I said sarcastically.

"Is there any particular significance to that name Parris, Aimee?" Dr. Strachey leaned over so he could see my eyes.

I glared back at him. "You know as well as I do,

Dr. Strachey, what the significance of the name Parris is! You undoubtedly read up on it last night!"

"This morning, really," said Dr. Strachey, smiling.

"And you know that it was at the home of the Reverend Samuel Parris in 1692 in Salem that the first of a series of young women were 'possessed' by the Devil!"

"I see," said Dr. Strachey.

"Elizabeth Parris was nine years old, and her cousin, Abigail Williams was eleven. The family slave, a Caribbean Indian named Tituba, would tell them lurid tales of the West Indies, filled with superstition. The girls were feverish and hysterical as they imagined all the weird things Tituba told them come true. And the tale went around the neighborhood—the girls were *bewitched*!"

I took a deep breath and lapsed into silence. I realized I had been making a fool of myself. But I was annoyed because I had told that story many times to people who were curious about Salem and curious about my name. Dr. Strachey was right: I was sick to death of morbid interest displayed in my connection with Salem, the witch town, the site of the great witch hunt of 1692. Yes. He was right, but I had suppressed my rage over it through the years and had pretended it meant nothing to me. So when Dr. Strachey had probed into my psyche, he had guessed at the truth, that I did not, indeed, like having come from Salem, that I did not, indeed, like to talk about witchcraft, that I did not, indeed, want ever to think of witches or of Salem or of my name Parris again.

He let the silence build up.

Then he said:

"When did you leave Salem?"

Facts again. I relaxed. "I left when I had finished college. Really a year *after* I graduated and returned there."

"And where did you go to college?"

"In Boston."

"I see. What did you do when you returned home?"

"I met Drew."

101

"Drew?"

"Drew Hanson. Actually, I always knew him. But I mean I met him under different circumstances. He was two years ahead of me in high school, and I knew him then. But when I got back from college, he was very much changed."

"Where did he go to college?"

"He didn't. There was never enough money."

"Why were you attracted to him?"

"Because he was a good person, very decent, and I had always liked his sister Angie."

"I see."

"Drew went to work after graduating from high school, driving a truck. By the time I had graduated from college, he had become a partner in the trucking firm, and was in charge of dispatching the trucks and allocating the freight loads. In other words, he was running the business, really, for the man who took him on as partner."

"And you fell in love with him?"

"We were engaged."

"And *then* you fell in love with him?"

"If I became engaged to him, I was in love with him, wasn't I?" I asked.

"I don't know. *Were* you? You're the one who's asking the question."

I lapsed into silence.

"Were you in love with him?" Dr. Strachey asked again.

I hesitated. "I think so. I wanted to marry him."

"It's hardly the same thing," chuckled Dr. Strachey.

"It's a foolish question, anyway! All this talk of sex and loose morals and—"

"Who's talking about loose morals?" Dr. Strachey interrupted. I could see a gleam in his eye.

"It goes with sex talk, doesn't it?" I asked.

"Does it?"

"Of course! If people weren't always talking about sex they wouldn't become involved in extra-marital relationships, would they?"

Dr. Strachey leaned forward, looking at me. "People

never discussed sex in the Victorian era, and yet in England the incidence of sex immorality was higher than in any other nation in history."

I flushed. "Now you're trying to embarrass me."

"Am I? Does the discussion of sex embarrass you?"

"No! But you're trying to make it so!"

"You're blushing."

"And so what if I am?" I blazed out.

"The fact that you are blushing means that you have inhibitions against the free discussion of sex."

"My mother and father taught me so!" I said. "I don't go around discussing sex and morals with everyone I meet."

"I'm sure you do not. Do you discuss it with your husband?"

I stared at him. "I don't like your attitude any more than your question, Dr. Strachey!"

"That means something. Then I assume that you do not discuss sex with your husband."

"We do not *need* to discuss it," I said hotly.

"Why not?"

"Because—because we—we have it—and that's enough!" I cried out, mortally chagrined that I had spoken of our private, innermost personal relations.

"I see," said Dr. Strachey. "The boy. Drew. Did you and he discuss sex?"

"No," I said softly.

"But certainly you engaged in a discussion of what your future would be as a married couple?"

"We simply—went together," I said softly.

"But in going together you must have had some sexual encounters. A kiss. A caress. Perhaps—more?"

"You're an evil, leering old man, Dr. Strachey!" I shouted, half rising from the couch.

"Am I?" he asked me, an enchanted look on his face. He scribbled on his lined pad furiously.

"Yes, you are!"

"What did your mother and father think about Drew?"

"They didn't like him," I said grudgingly, annoyed now at my parents, and not Dr. Strachey.

"And why not?"

"They said Drew was 'beneath me.' You know, all that parental snobbery bunk."

"How did Drew react to this?"

"He simply laughed at them. He said he wanted me. He said he wasn't marrying them. It was all very horrible."

"Horrible? I think Drew had the right idea. Don't you?"

I stared at him as he leaned over to look at me. "Of course not! Your parents are your family! If I had married Drew and renounced my parents, I would have been a most thankless child!"

"Yes, I agree," said Dr. Strachey thoughtfully. "But he was right, wasn't he? He was marrying you, and not marrying your family."

I said nothing.

"Did your parents ever discuss sex with you?"

I frowned. "What has that got to do——?"

"Answer me."

"No."

"Why not?"

"They are very modest people, Dr. Strachey! Very modest people! They do not believe in boasting about their sexual exploits or in discussing the more private concerns of a person's inner life. Sex is a private and very personal thing. It is not to be bruited about."

"I agree completely," said Dr. Strachey. "Still, most parents discuss the elementals of sex with their children."

"Not in my family," I said.

"I see," said Dr. Strachey.

"You may see, but Drew didn't see," I said, suddenly letting the whole past flood in on me. "He hated them for their prudery. He hated the way I pulled away from him whenever he began to make love to me. It was terribly embarrassing, really! He was simply——"

I stopped.

"He was simply——what?" Dr. Strachey prompted me.

"Too 'earthy,' too 'worldy' for me," I confessed, and I could feel the hot tears coming to my eyes. I remembered with shame the scene between my parents and me when we had discussed the situation and later when I had told Drew that I was leaving Salem to move to New York and breaking my engagement to him.

Dr. Strachey nodded.

"He would have married me, Dr. Strachey," I said tearfully. "But my father declared the engagement dissolved. He told Drew not to try to run off with me, because he would have the law on him. And Drew—"

"What did Drew do?"

"Drew told him he had nothing to do with the two of us. But I loved my father. I love him now. I told Drew that I couldn't marry him if it meant hurting my father. And so that was the reason I left Salem."

"Your parents forced you to leave!"

I nodded silently.

"Do you hate them?"

"No. I love them. It just wasn't working out. When I married Don, they had no objections."

"Did they ever meet Don?"

"Only once. At the wedding."

"I see," said Dr. Strachey.

"And I *am* loved, Dr. Strachey," I cried out, angered at his badgering, angered at myself for my lack of emotional control. "I *am* loved! By my parents! By Drew! By Don!"

"I'm sure you are, Aimee," Dr. Strachey said. "But I am not so sure you *believe* you are."

"What's *that* mean?" I sobbed.

He shook his head and consulted his watch.

Our time was up.

Chapter Ten

At the first opportunity I drew Jill Towers aside and took her into my office. Jill was openly curious as to what I wanted to discuss with her, but she did not ask me directly.

"Jill," I said, pulling out a folder with her background notes in it, "you've been here at Fairfield Residence Hall for a year and a half. Is that right?"

"Yes, Mrs. Hammond," she said. She was a pleasant blonde girl with a wind-blown, outdoor look.

"Do you like it here?"

A flash of interest crossed her eyes, but then vanished. She was a bit more mature than she looked, I reasoned. Nineteen, her dossier said. She was going to the Coldwater branch of the state university.

"Certainly, Mrs. Hammond. Why do you ask?"

I looked her square in the eye. "The death of Lora Blake has upset everyone, Jill. She took her life apparently because of some great fear she had. I am simply trying to find out if there is some evil or aggravating influence here at the Hall that I do not know about."

"Evil influence?" Jill repeated, a half smile on her pretty mouth.

"Lora Blake committed suicide, Jill. I realize she could have been suicidally inclined even before she came here. But something set her off. I'm seriously trying to find out what that—*influence*—was." I had to find out how deeply she was involved.

"I see," Jill said. "I was there with her, fighting to

keep her from going out the window, Mrs. Hammond. I have no idea *what* was driving her."

"How did you discover that she was attempting to jump?" I asked suddenly. "In all the excitement at the time, believe I never did hear."

Jill stared over my shoulder. "She became upset in her room, Mrs. Hammond. She called me in. And in the midst of a quiet conversation, she suddenly rose from her bed, ran out through the door, and went into Mrs. Venefica's office."

"And where was Mrs. Venefica?"

"I don't know." Jill frowned. "I think she was in one of the rooms. Lying down, I believe. She said later she felt ill."

"There is a bed in her own office," I suggested.

Jill shook her head. "I don't know why she wasn't in her office, Mrs. Hammond. When Lora ran there, I followed her. I caught up to her in Mrs. Venefica's office and—"

"Did she saying anything to you?"

"Say anything?" Jill thought back.

"Yes. When she leaped up and ran out of her room?"

"Oh. It was something about Benjy. That was her boy friend, Mrs. Hammond. Benjy Petersen. He died in a car accident recently."

"Then she was upset over Benjy's death?"

"I don't know, Mrs. Hammond. She rarely spoke about him. She was very quiet."

"You thought she might be on the verge of hysteria, and you followed her. Is that it?"

"Yes, Mrs. Hammond. In Mrs. Venefica's office she tried to get away from me. I grabbed at her. She kept screaming for someone to help her. 'Help me!' she kept crying."

"Help her—what?" I asked Jill.

She shook her head. "I never found out. When you came in the door, I turned to see who it was, and Lora broke away from me. She climbed up into the window and went out."

Yes. I recalled the scene, vividly. That was exactly

107

how it had been. It was time to call Jill's bluff—her pretense that there was nothing out-of-the-way happening on the fourth floor.

"Do you think it was the rituals, Jill?"

She turned a wide-eyed, innocent face to me. "Rituals?"

I recalled the similar blankness in the face of Lora Blake herself the day of her death when I had met her on the first floor. That was the time she had denied coming out to my house and asking me to take her to Kennedy Airport. Had she really not remembered? And Jill?

"Come now, Jill. I know it's only a game. But I'm interested. I mean, the magic circle."

Jill looked at me a moment. Then she glanced away, moistened her lip with her tongue, and began to whisper: "What magic circle?"

"There *is* a magic circle, is there not?" I said evenly.

"I never heard about it, Mrs. Hammond," Jill said steadily. I could not be sure she was lying.

"I have," I snapped. "I've heard that Mrs. Venefica has been having magic sessions with the lot of you on the fourth floor. She told me so herself. You've got a nice little witch's coven there!"

Jill smiled. "Witches? There's no such thing as witches—except on television, Mrs. Hammond!"

"Lora Blake was a very unsophisticated young girl," I said to Jill Towers angrily. "She was extremely suggestive. And I have a feeling that the rituals you went through frightened her to death. She was a devout young girl, who believed in the Bible. With your witches coven, however innocent it might have been, you could have pushed her over the edge of sanity."

"But there was no witchcraft," Jill said flatly. "Someone has been lying to you." She looked very indignant.

Indeed, yes, I thought. Someone was lying. Jill Towers. Or was she lying? Was her mind her own?

I excused her after I had tried several more times to shake her story, and then went on to Patience Thompson. But I got the same result from her. And so on

108

down the list of girls on the fourth floor, until I came to Doreen Gray.

Doreen was twenty-one, and also a student of the Coldwater Branch of the state university. She was dark-haired with green eyes and a white skin that had to be protected from sunshine. She was tall and well-built and had an intelligent and self-assured way about her.

"Now you've been here for two years, Doreen, isn't that right?"

"Yes, Mrs. Hammond." There was a faint smile on her curved lips. "And this is the first time I've had a little chat like this with the Assistant Manager of the Hall."

I could not help but laugh. "All right, Doreen. It *is* unusual. But this is a serious situation."

Doreen's face sobered. "What is? Lora Blake's death?"

I nodded.

Doreen bit her lip. "It was going to happen, you know. I told them that, and it turned out exactly as I had suspected."

"You *suspected* Lora was sick?"

Doreen frowned. "Oh, I've taken a psychology course or two. Yes, I did suspect."

"Why didn't you come to me or Mrs. Grant?"

The girl shook her head. "It simply didn't seem that bad. You know, I thought she would get over it."

"Why do you think she was disturbed?"

"Her boy friend. What was his name?"

"Benjy Petersen."

"Right. She was broken up about him. And not having any parents, you know—it left her wide open to hallucinations."

I straightened. "Hallucinations?"

"Yes. Because of the games."

"Games?" Now we were getting to the crux of the matter.

Doreen stared at me with narrowed eyes. "That's what you called me in for, isn't it? To find out about the games?"

"I had heard they were *rituals*." Best to "lay it on the line," as they say.

"Actually they are. It's just fun stuff out of books and magazines, Mrs. Hammond. You know all that talk about witches and witchcraft. We were just playing a game."

So Doreen *did* remember. And the chances were that Jill remembered too, and had lied to me.

"All of you?" I asked.

"The twelve of us on the fourth floor. That makes a coven. We had been getting along with eleven, until Lora came. She was perfect to fill in the twelfth place."

"Had this been going on before you came to the Hall?" I asked, thinking about Don's story of the garroted girl.

"No," Doreen replied. "In fact, Mrs. Venefica only started it up this year in the spring. At Beltane."

"Beltane?"

"Yes. May first. That's the night the witches ride. Four times a year, Mrs. Hammond. Beltane or May Day. May first. Lammas or Lugnassad. August first. Hallows. November first. And Brigid or Candlemas. February first. Every quarter." Doreen smiled broadly. "It's all a lot of nonsense really, but it's fun. It's a game."

"Don't you realize that your 'game' may have been the inadvertant cause of Lora Blake's death?"

Doreen's face paled. She looked down. "When it happened I tried not to think about it. And Mrs. Venefica swore us all to eternal silence. If we told anyone, she said, the spell would suck the spirits out of our bodies."

"Why didn't you volunteer this information to me?"

Doreen considered. "I thought someone would be asking us pretty soon. I just wondered—"

"No more of this, do you understand?" I said, much the same way I had said it to Mrs. Venefica. "No more! Now tell the girls I know all about this and that you're not to do any of it again! I've already had a chat with Mrs. Venefica. You hear me?"

I stood up and glared at the girl.

110

She slowly rose, eyes lowered. I let her out.

For a moment I debated whether or not to tell Mrs. Grant immediately what I now knew about Mrs. Venefica and the girls on the fourth floor. At the last moment, I lifted the phone to dial her, and discovered that she was out of the Hall for the afternoon. She was making a visit to one of the Hall's patrons in an attempt to raise money for the next year's budget.

So I went up the stairs to Mrs. Venefica's office myself, to tell her I had spoken to the girls about the witchcraft sessions and had told them never to repeat the rituals. It was at that point that I had one of those flashes of intuition—or, probably, in my case, a vagrant memory had surfaced—and I stopped in the middle of the steps and returned to the ground floor. There was a small library just past Mrs. Grant's office, and I went in there to look at the reference books. Yes. There was one: a Latin dictionary.

I put it down on the table and opened it to the V's.

And there it was.

As big as life.

Venefica. "Witch."

Venefica meant "witch" in Latin! The fool woman had changed her name to Venefica to make herself into a witch! Or perhaps her twisted old mind had thought that she would be better able to chant rituals and perform magic if she had a witch's name!

No matter.

I slammed the book shut, put it back on the shelf, and marched out into the hallway and up the stairs. I was simmering with rage, trying to keep myself from boiling over, although I knew that the old woman was a pitiable object at best. But she had been so diabolically *clever*—taunting us with such an obvious hint at her real "game."

I should have laughed—there were elements of humor in the situation. But I was so angry to have been hoodwinked for so long, that I failed to see the humor of the matter at that moment.

I myself held to no belief in witches or in witchcraft

or in the Devil. But I knew what a misguided belief in the occult could do to people. Ben had told me about that.

Lora Blake, because she was young and not very bright, had begun to *believe* in witchcraft, and she had frightened herself to death and taken her life to keep from being a victim of the Devil's torments.

Foolish old woman! And stupid young girls, to have been misled by her!

Stretched to my full height, I rapped angrily on her office door. The door moved slightly inward, and I realized it was not latched. I peered through the widening crack into the office and froze.

Someone was lying on the floor!

I pushed in and saw Mrs. Venefica stretched out on her side, slumped into what seemed to be the posture of death, neither breathing nor moving.

I leaned down over her, reaching instantly for her wrist and pressing my ear to her breast.

A faint murmur.

Quickly I dialed Dr. Kingsley.

He came in minutes. We were all crowded into the small infirmary on the second floor around Mrs. Venefica. The girls had helped me carry her down there.

And Dr. Kingsley made us all go outside while he worked on her.

It was half an hour later that he sat with me in my office downstairs and had a cup of coffee from the kitchen.

"She's resting comfortably," he told me as he sipped the brew.

That was what doctors always said. "What was wrong with her?"

"She had a mild heart attack," said Dr. Kingsley slowly. "That is what it would be called in layman's terms, anyway."

"Thank you, Doctor," I said stiffly. "What is the prognosis?"

He set the coffee cup down. "Oh, one or two more, perhaps, and then—" He lifted his right hand and snapped his fingers in the air.

"She may—die?" I asked softly.

"She's an old woman," said Dr. Kingsley with a smile. "You think she will live forever?"

I wondered how much I should tell Dr. Kingsley. I thought perhaps I should tell him everything.

"Where can we put her?" I asked without preamble.

"Why, in her bed, of course. That's where she is now."

I shook my head. "No, Doctor. I mean after. I don't think she's doing our girls much good."

"She never did," Dr. Kingsley chuckled. "But it's kept her out of mischief."

I leaned forward. "Dr. Kingsley, Mrs. Venefica—or whatever her name is—is indirectly responsible for the death of Lora Blake last week. And I—"

"How do you know?"

As briefly as I could, I told him what Doreen Gray had said to me.

He sat there absorbing the information and pursing his lips. When I had finished he took up the cup of coffee and drank some more.

"I warn you against moving her out," he said. He was adamant.

"But why? Doctor, don't you realize the seriousness of the situation? If another girl—?"

"Are any others particularly *susceptible*?"

"No," I answered.

"You can keep your eyes on Mrs. Venefica. She won't give you any trouble."

"I want her out of here!"

He shook his head. "I do not recommend removal. Any such thing would surely bring about her own death."

I stared at him in shock. "Do you mean she too is that close to death?"

He smiled faintly. "She is on a very thin edge, Mrs. Hammond. Now. Do you want to push her over?"

I sat back, stunned to learn that Mrs. Venefica was actually a dying woman. I did not know what to do now.

"I would simply let her stay there, where she is, secure and safe, and let time take its course. You can't seriously believe that any harm can come to the girls, can you?" Dr. Kingsley's eyes were mocking.

"Are you saying you do not believe that Mrs. Venefica's little games had anything to do with Lora Blake's death?"

He sat there and watched me a long moment. Finally, he said, "Poppycock!"

"You don't believe?"

"Of course, I don't believe in witchcraft or witches! It's nonsense! No one does!"

"I don't either! But—Lora Blake *did*!"

"Something else was troubling her, Mrs. Hammond. Please. Let's not waste time arguing. You asked me what I recommended for Mrs. Venefica. I say, keep her on here. Let her rest. Home is the best place to die."

I stared at him.

He picked up his little black bag, swung toward the door, and then paused.

"It will come out all right in the end, Mrs. Hammond," he said lightly. "Try not to worry *yourself* into a breakdown."

That reminded me that he was the one who had sent me to Dr. Strachey.

"I'll try," I said irritably.

Smiling, he left the Hall.

I tiptoed in on Mrs. Venefica a half hour later. She was sleeping very soundly, breaking into a loud snore every now and then. Even when I turned on the light she did not waken. I moved over to the door, and glanced out into the hallway. There was no one in sight. And I knew that no one had seen me come up here.

I closed the door and got the notebook out of my bag, along with the pencil. It was the first opportunity I had ever had to explore Mrs. Venefica's office thoroughly. It was, as I had suspected, a clutter of many different kinds of things: papers, magazines, boxes of trinkets, plant food, plants, and old clothes of all kinds.

First, I took the notebook I had brought along and

drew a picture of each of the plants growing in the room. There were fifteen of them, and each was different. I did not recognize one of them; but then, I have never pretended to be a botanist.

Then I went through her papers, but discovered they were pitifully few. I could not find any kind of identification that had her name on it, leading me to believe that she had chosen the name Venefica from the Latin dictionary.

I went through her clothes, but there were no unusual gowns, except for one cape that a witch might wear during a coven meeting. I threw it aside.

And then, on the bottom of the closet floor I found the treasure trove of books—dozens of volumes dealing with witchcraft, demonology, and spell-casting, including one on cooking up philtres and on making potions for all kinds of spells.

I clutched those books in my hands and stared at them, wishing I had time at that moment to study them, but knowing that I had better leave as soon as possible. Then, to my shock, I heard a rap at the door.

"Who's in there?" a voice asked.

I recognized Mary Leland.

"It's only me, Mary," I said, putting the books on the desk, and opening the door a tiny slit.

"How is Mrs. Venefica?" Mary asked, trying to see past me.

"Fine. I'm just tidying up for her," I said.

"Oh," said Mary.

I shut the door in her face.

Five minutes later, I opened the door, saw no one there, and moved stealthily out into the hall, carrying the books and the sketches I had made. No one saw me as I went rapidly down the stairs and put them in my office, in a bag, to take to Ben Magruder that night.

Ben was up and about, although still weak, with that obnoxious Mrs. Bensonhurst skulking about in the living room making life unbearable for Don and me. But I gave Ben the sketches and the books, and his eyes lighted up. I told him briefly about Mrs. Venefica, and he smiled when I came to the part about the Latin dictionary.

"Don't tell me you knew that already!" I snapped.

"Of course, I knew!" Ben laughed. "But it has nothing to do with whether or not she's a witch! A witch can use a simple subterfuge like that to throw off those who wish to penetrate her real identity. And an innocent person can take on such a name to *pretend*."

"In other words, it doesn't prove a thing about her?"

"Nothing," said Ben. His eyes narrowed. "But that doesn't mean there *isn't* a witch at that Hall!"

"One of the girls too?"

"Which one?" Ben sighed. He cleared his throat. "I've been studying some of the records at the Town Hall, you know—about that garroting and so on. I think I may have news for you soon, Aimee."

"News about what?" Don asked.

"About who's trying to put the spell on you, Aimee, and *why*."

"Spell?"

"The dreams," Ben said. "I have a brand new theory!"

I looked at him blankly.

"Let's go, Don," I said, and we left. I looked back once and saw Ben watching me strangely.

"I can always plan counter-measures!" he cried out after me.

He was quite cute and quite mad, I thought. I went home and went to bed. I abandoned myself to Don.

It was a strange evening.

Chapter Eleven

It was a foolish thing for Don to get angry over, but there he stood, almost beside himself, holding out his old tie clasp to me.

He was shouting so vehemently that I could barely make out the words.

"What is the matter, Don?" I asked impatiently, coming out of the kitchen, where I was trying to finish dinner, and confronting him in the hallway outside our bedroom.

"My tie clip! Where is it? I told you I needed one!"

I was so taken aback by his verbal attack on me that I could not think of anything to say.

"Well, Aimee! Well?"

"Well, what, Don? My goodness! I'll get you one as soon as I find the time for it!" I frowned. "I know you broke yours a week ago. I'm going to get a new one for you. I said I would."

"I could get it myself!" snapped Don. "It would take a hell of a lot less time!"

"Then why don't you?" I flared.

"Because you said you were going to buy me a new one today at Wagner's in Coldwater! That's why I've waited. I've been walking around with a loose necktie for four days now, and I've about had enough of it!"

"As soon as I replace my brooch," I said, trying to keep my temper in check. "I told you that, Don."

Don smiled bleakly. "That's what makes me mad, Aimee! You've replaced your brooch—and where is my tie clip?"

117

"I—" Don was standing there, hands on his hips, with a self-satisfied look on his face, and I knew I had better watch what I was going to say. I recognized that self-righteous look and knew that he was going to "teach me a lesson." My heart sank.

"Before you say anything, Aimee," Don said, his voice dropping to a very low, intimate rumble, "look at this." He put out the other hand under my nose and opened it, palm up. In it lay a brand new brooch.

"But, Don," I said, looking at him in dismay. "What is it?"

"That's the new brooch you bought yourself!" he snapped. "I found it on your dresser! That's why I blew my top about the tie clip! Why did you forget it, when you promised?"

I stared at him, at a loss for words. I could not for the life of me remember going to Wagner's, and if I had, I could not remember buying myself the brooch that Don was holding out to me. Yet it was a nice, simple little thing, exactly the kind of trinket I would buy for myself. I reached out and took it in my hand and examined it carefully.

Don watched with a supercilious smile. "I suppose next you're going to tell me you never saw it before! Never bought it!"

I was afraid to answer.

"Well? Aimee?"

"Yes," I said spiritedly. "That's exactly what I am going to say. That I did not buy it and that I never even saw it before. I didn't forget your tie clip, I simply never went to Wagner's at all."

Don frowned, for a moment nonplussed. "Well, I suppose it's nothing to make such a big fuss about," he admitted. "Here. Give it to me, and I'll put it back in your things."

I gave it to him and he put it away. Five minutes later, we were eating dinner and the incident was forgotten.

Don wanted the news about the Hall, and I told him about Mrs. Venefica's heart attack, and about questioning the girls over the "witches game" they had been playing. He was startled that they had been playing it, and he cautioned me to make sure they never did it again. I told him that with Mrs. Venefica in bed, there would be no chance of that.

"Make sure there isn't, or I'm going to get you out of that place!" Don vowed.

We were through dessert when the phone rang and I heard Ben Magruder on the other end.

"Where were you?" he asked in a suppressed voice.

"At the Hall. Then here at home. Why?" I did not know what he was talking about.

"I called you! I called you from the Town Hall this afternoon."

"No one told me, Ben," I said to calm him. "I'm sorry. They're usually very good about giving me messages."

"Oh, come now, Aimee!" he said harshly. "Don't try to put me on! You talked to me yourself! You promised to come right over to the Town Hall to look at what I had uncovered there!"

"Ben," I said, "I have no idea what you're talking about."

There was a pause. "Are you all right, Aimee?" he asked cautiously.

"Certainly I'm all right! Why do you ask?"

"Aimee, I talked to you for five minutes on the phone and you promised to get right over to the Town Hall to meet me, and you never showed up! I want to know what's wrong with you!"

"There's nothing wrong with me, and I think you're lying!" I was beginning to lose my temper once again.

"Are you sure?" Ben asked me in an incredulous tone of voice.

"I'm very sure!" I snapped.

"I see," he said in a vague, far-off voice.

"What is it all about, Ben?" I asked. "I mean, what did you find at the Town Hall?"

"It's—it's nothing," he said softly. "I'll show it to you tomorrow."

"All right, Ben." I frowned. "Are *you* all right?"

"Certainly!" he growled. "Look, can you put Don on, please?"

"I suppose so," I said coldly. "Don't you want to talk to me any more, Ben?"

"Certainly, dearest, but just let me speak to Don for a moment."

I nodded and turned. Don was standing there behind me, watching me with some concern.

"It's Ben," I said. "He's angry with me. You talk to him!"

I stalked out into the kitchen.

Through the open door I could hear Don on the telephone.

"Sure, Ben. Yeah. She's all right. A little absent-minded, but that's all . . . What? . . . I said, a little absent-minded, but that's all . . . She forgot to get me a new tie clip and I've been walking around for a week with my tie blowing up into my face. I turned on the heat tonight and she's miffed. It's my fault . . . No. She said she forgot. And she must have. She bought herself a brooch and forgot to buy my tie clip . . . Huh? I never knew she did that. When? . . . I don't think so, Ben. Why? . . . It *is* important? Well, I suppose."

I heard Don's footsteps coming into the kitchen. I turned so my back was to him when he came in the room, but he paid no attention to my boorishness.

"Aimee, what did you send to Ben?"

"Nothing," I said quietly.

"Are you sure you didn't send him something by mail?"

"Of course I didn't send him anything by mail," I responded, turning now and facing Don. I was beginning to wonder if the entire world was populated with weirdos. "I always telephone him!"

"He says you sent a package. Do you know what's in the package?"

I shook my head dazedly. "Do you mean to say Ben has received a package from me?"

"Yes. It was sent by messenger from the Hall."

"Ben says that?"

"Yes."

"Why didn't he tell *me*?" I asked flatly.

"He said he was annoyed with you about standing him up this afternoon. Why did you do *that*, Aimee?"

"Ben is mistaken, dear. He did not call me. I did not talk to him. He's making it up."

"Why would he make it up, Aimee?" Don wondered.

"I don't know. Probably just another lie—" I remembered the package. "What does the package look like?" I asked.

"Why don't you talk to Ben?" Don asked.

I went in and got on the phone. "Ben?"

"Yes, Aimee."

"I did *not* send you anything by mail."

"But it's your handwriting—I mean, my address is in your hand, and, so is the return address."

"Someone has forged it, Ben."

"I don't like it, Aimee." His voice dropped in timbre. "There's something very strange going on at the Hall."

I stared into the telephone handset. A package sent from the Hall by me? Never!

"Ben, you'd better not open that package—I mean, if you're suspicious of it!"

"I've already opened it, Aimee."

"What was in the box?"

"A reel of tape, Aimee."

"Tape? Did you play it?"

"There's more. I have a note in your handwriting, Aimee. Listen. 'I heard this incantation in the Hall on the fourth floor, Ben. Can you interpret it? It's becoming more and more frightening here every day. What should I do? Aimee.'"

I laughed into the phone. "That's what the note says? I never wrote that!"

"I know your handwriting, Aimee," Ben cautioned.

"I didn't write it," I insisted.

"I played the tape, Aimee."

"And what did you hear?" I asked, half-afraid of what the answer might be.

Ben gave a little chuckle. "Interestingly enough,

Aimee, there's not a word on the tape. It's been erased!"

I turned to stare at Don. "Erased?"

"Yes," said Ben. "So I guess I'll have to pass up the incantation. Sorry, Aimee."

"Ben, someone is trying to play a joke on you," I said. "I did not send that tape! I did hear an incantation, but I told you about that. I never taped it."

"Not that you remember, anyway. Right?"

"Right. Not that I remember."

"Aimee, enough of this talk for now. I'm going to the Town Hall again tomorrow. There are a lot of important files I want to to go through. I think I've found out who's behind this, and why it's being done! It's an absolutely sensational story!"

"Tell me now!" I pleaded. "Unless it's all mere speculation!"

"No. This is fact," said Ben.

"I don't believe any of it!" I snapped. "It's just a game—a silly game!"

"Get a good night's rest and prepare yourself for an interesting afternoon tomorrow, Aimee! Good night!"

And he had hung up before I could plead for more information.

Don was absolutely adamant.

"You've got to get out of that place, Aimee. I know now why you've been so absent-minded, so devoid of interest in me, so totally different these past few weeks. They've put some kind of spell on you!"

I whipped around on him unbelievingly. "You, Don? Old Mr. Nuts and Bolts Hammond? Come now! Don't tell me you've begun to think the way Ben Magruder does!"

I was scoffing, but I could hear my voice tremble. I was not quite so sure about myself as I pretended to be.

"I don't believe in what Ben believes in any more than you do, Aimee," he said, "but there's something wrong with you. And it all started when you went to work at the Hall."

"There is nothing wrong at all!"

"What about Lora Blake's death?" asked Don with flat practicality.

I stared at him. "That's not fair, Don. You know I had nothing to do with that! The poor girl—"

"What *did* happen that night, Aimee? Did you take her to Kennedy Airport? Did you put her on the plane? How did she get back to the Hall, Aimee?" Don stared at me. "Or did you turn right around and drive her to the Hall when she got in the car, Aimee?"

There was a long silence.

"Don, what are you talking about?"

"You're not yourself, Aimee," he said sadly. "I don't know what's wrong with you, but I know you haven't been *you*. I think you drove poor Lora Blake back to the Hall that night, and lied to me when you said you went to Kennedy."

"Why would I lie?" I asked.

"Why would you drive her back to the Hall?" Don asked. "I don't know. And I think you don't know, either. That's what worries me. There are too many strange things going on here. And now this thing with Ben Magruder."

I stared at Don. "Do you believe Ben, or do you believe me?"

Don hesitated. "I would believe you all the way, Aimee, if it weren't for that tie clip you didn't buy me. I don't know what made you forget, but it must have been something very important. And I don't even know if you *did* forget. I think maybe you drew a blank on the whole afternoon!"

I sank back in the chair. "Don, please!"

"I think you drew a blank on that Kennedy trip, too. I think you drew a blank on that shopping trip today to Wagner's. And I believe you may have drawn a blank on that tape you sent Ben."

"I've been tired," I admitted, putting my hand over my forehead. I was numb all over. I could not think straight.

"I see it this way," Don went on, warming up to the subject. "I think those girls on the fourth floor were in it with Mrs. Venefica all the time. I think they were playing a game, the game of witches. All right. It was great sport. But then something went wrong. And Lora Blake killed herself because she was frightened out of her skull of being 'possessed' after something had happened at one of the magic rites. Do you follow me, Aimee?"

I nodded weakly.

"Right. And then the witches' circle panicked after Lora died. They tried to sweep the whole thing under the carpet. But it wouldn't stay buried. I think the excitement of the thing gave Mrs. Venefica a heart attack. And then, when you tried to question them all about the rituals, the girls withdrew even further and pretended nothing had ever happened. And now—"

I shook my head. "I don't believe it, Don."

"No? Well, listen some more. I think they got to you some way. I don't know how, and I don't believe in that sort of thing. But from the first, ever since you've worked at the Hall, you've been different, Aimee! I mean—*different*. Those dreams you said you had. I don't know if they were really dreams or not. I think they're more like hallucinations! And they turned you into a wanton woman! Not that I mind a wanton woman once in a while, but, Aimee, it wasn't you! You were someone else—someone of the flesh! A—a witch, damn it! Don't you see? They had you under a spell from the first!"

I closed my eyes. "Don, please—"

"And I think Ben Magruder's right. I think they put you under a spell because you're doubly susceptible. First. You came from Salem. That means you're automatically knowledgeable about witchcraft, at least in theory. Second. Your name is Parris, a direct descendent of one of the Salem girls! Somehow you psyched yourself into a spell, Aimee, or you were under one. And that accounts for the blackouts. The lapses. The nightmares."

I stared at him, my eyes blurring. I could not see him well at all, and I began to feel the heat rising within me.

"And I think today you did hear the rites being carried on. I think you made a tape recording of them. I think you did intend to send it to Ben Magruder. But at the last moment, something happened, maybe something inside you. Or maybe they put a spell on you. And you simply *erased the tape yourself!*"

I gawked at him, and it was like looking through the wrong end of a telescope. He was growing dimmer and dimmer.

"And then when you went over to buy my tie clip you were so worried, you drew a blank again. Later, when you came back, you got a telephone call from Ben, and promised him you would come right over. But the minute you hung up, you decided not to. And you wiped it out of your mind."

"But, Don, what can I do about it?" I asked feebly. I could barely see him at all now. It was growing dark everywhere.

"I don't know!" Don said. "But I'm not going to let you go back to that Hall ever again. Do you hear me?"

I could not answer. Then quite suddenly, I was alert and myself once again.

"Don," I said. "I must return to the Hall. I must work with Ben to find out what's going on there and to stop it! I'm the only one who can do it, Don. You must let me!"

He stared at me a moment and then paced back and forth. I was somewhat surprised that he had not blown up at me. Finally, he came to a stop in front of me, and gazed at me reflectively.

"I understand what you're trying to do, Aimee, and I admire you for your courage. I suppose it does come to that—that you are the only one who can really find out what is going on there and help put a stop to it." He walked back and forth a bit more. "Well, if Ben thinks you can do something about it, I can't stand in your way. I'm not in favor of it—don't get me wrong about that—but I know if I try to stop you, you'll come at me with all the male chauvinist arguments in the world and shove them down my throat. Right now, I don't need any of that!"

125

I smiled and rose, throwing my arms around his neck. "Darling!" I cried. "Of course! Don't you see—it's got to be that way?"

He said nothing, but squeezed me tighter.

And I felt the heat move through me. I felt like laughing in triumph, but I did not.

Chapter Twelve

There is nothing to be gained by pretending I was not confused, frightened, and apprehensive about the situation at Fairfield Residence Hall. I had been bluffing when I talked to Don. I think Don realized I was bluffing, and he himself was somewhat frightened too.

I tried to puzzle it all out next morning, at the same time trying to accomplish my chores and keep the job going at the Hall. I could not understand how I had been able to buy myself a brooch at Wagner's, and not buy Don his tie clip. And then, more than that, I did not understand how I had purchased the brooch without being able to remember!

And there was that peculiar conversation with Ben Magruder that I was *supposed* to have carried on by telephone. I simply had no recollection of it. I half hoped that Ben Magruder might be playing some kind of joke on me, but somehow it did not seem likely—although it would certainly be in character if he had. He was always trying to unsettle me.

As for the tape, where could I have gotten it? Where was there a tape recorder in the Hall? I sat there a moment in indecision, and then pressed a button. Jill Towers came in.

"Yes, Mrs. Hammond?" She was properly respectful, and quite impersonal. It was as if our little discussion the other day had never occurred.

"I'd like to use a tape recorder. Does the Hall have one?"

"Of course, Mrs. Hammond. In the basement. We use it sometimes for group singing."

"I see," I said as steadily as I could manage. Group incantation! "Could you bring it to me?"

She nodded. "Right away."

It was a portable affair, easily carried, using regular-sized reels of tape. Jill Towers set it up on my desk, showed me how to open it, and started to go.

"Can you show me how it works?"

She obliged, and began to load the reels.

"That's funny," she said. "There are only two full reels. The empty and one blank."

"Is there something wrong with that?" I said.

"We always keep two blanks in the case, if we need an extra."

I stared at the case in front of me. I could barely find my tongue. "All right, Jill. Thank you very much."

She went out.

I stared at the machine for a long moment and pushed the PLAY button. Then quickly, I pushed the STOP button and rose from my chair, crossed the room and closed the door to my office. When I returned to my seat, I turned on the PLAY button again, and listened.

The tape was blank.

I have no idea what I expected to hear—the incantations from the fourth floor, perhaps, or maybe something even more sinister.

But there was nothing.

I turned off the machine and sat there deeply perplexed. It had become obvious that somehow I had been forced to forget several specific acts I had performed the day before. How? Had my own psyche rejected them from my memory? Or had something outside my own person erased these acts from my mind, much the same way a tape recorder can erase words from a full reel?

My mind turned to Ben Magruder's warnings. Was someone deliberately trying to "steal my own mind," much the same as he, she, or it had stolen Lora Blake's will power? Was it true that my own blackouts and lapses of memory were controlled from outside me? Had it something to do with my name? My background? My involvement with Salem?

In the cold light of day I could hardly believe anything quite so sinister and weird. But I had to admit that something had been happening to me—something that was unusual and not really explainable. At least not explainable to me!

I went to the window and stared out at the street. I could see the shoppers going into Wagner's across the street, others walking back and forth from one office building to another, still others simply standing and chatting with acquaintances.

No. This was Coldwater, not Salem. This was the twentieth century, not the seventeenth. Witches and witchcraft were simply products of the imagination, not realities.

But I remembered Ben Magruder's old theme: Perhaps you do not believe in witchcraft yourself, but if someone else does, it *can* exist for him, and for anyone else who believes.

But I did *not* believe. Therefore, how could I be affected?

As I sat there another alternative suggested itself, and I blinked my eyes in surprise.

Did I really not believe?

Perhaps—subconsciously—I *did* believe.

And that would make all the difference in the world.

Dr. Strachey was not much help. I did not tell him my own suspicions at all. I simply went to him for my second appointment, and he led me in, chatting innocuously, and had me relax on the couch again.

"Have you thought over what we discussed two days ago?" he asked me gently.

"Not really," I said.

"I thought you might have gotten some insight into yourself," he mused pleasantly.

"Perhaps I did," I answered.

"Did you like Salem?" he asked.

"Of course."

"Have you been back since you married?"

"No."

"Yet you hold no animosity toward your mother and father because of their enmity to—" he glanced at his notes—"Drew Hanson?"

"None," I said.

"Yet, of course, you are sensitive about Salem. The witches, I mean."

"Yes," I said. "I told you that."

"Do most of the people of Salem feel that way?"

"I don't think so," I said thoughtfully. "No."

"Why do you feel more sensitive than they?"

"I suppose because of my name. Parris."

"All right," he said. "What happened to the original house of the witch? Or should I say, the house of the 'possessed' girls?"

"It still stands."

"Did you visit it much?"

"Never," I said.

"I see," said Dr. Strachey. "Did most of the people of Salem stay away from it?"

"No. I think most everyone goes up to see the witch house at least once."

"But you did not?"

"No."

"Why are you afraid of the witch house?"

"I was not afraid of it, Dr. Strachey."

"No? Then why did you stay away?"

"I simply did not want to see it. Have you ever seen the Statue of Liberty, Dr. Strachey?"

"I'm afraid not."

"But you've been in New York, haven't you?"

"I was born there."

"You see?"

"It isn't really the same thing, Aimee, although I will admit it is a good parallel."

"I find nothing significant in the fact that I did not visit the witch house."

"However, I do," said Dr. Strachey.

"Tell me why, then," I said.

"Later, perhaps."

"Now, please!" I said, my voice rising. "Dr. Strachey, I am all mixed up about things that have been happening to me. I have a feeling some of my confusion may be because of my Salem background. Can you please tell me what you mean?"

There was silence. Finally: "What has been happening to you, Aimee?"

I was fuming at him for not answering my question. But finally, I decided I would play his game.

"I have done things I cannot remember doing," I said.

He glanced at me briefly. "What kind of things?"

"Simple things. I bought myself a brooch."

"What kind of brooch?"

"A simple brooch. Junk jewelry, you would call it."

"Have you any idea why you might want to hide the fact from yourself?"

"No," I said. "I only found out about it when I forgot to buy my husband a tie clip."

"A tie clip," mused Dr. Strachey.

"And I do not remember a conversation I had with a friend of mine."

"Who was this friend?"

"A man named Ben Magruder."

"Is he a good friend?"

"Yes."

"A lover?"

"Nonsense!" I said, rising and looking at Dr. Strachey with a fiery eye. "He's old enough to be my father. Or grandfather!"

"That means nothing," said Dr. Strachey glibly.

"He is not a lover!"

"What did he want to talk about?"

I hesitated. "He never did tell me."

"Come now. You know what he was calling for. I can tell by the way you hesitate. Why are you blocking?"

"All right! He called me to tell me he had found out something about the Fairfield Residence Hall."

"What about it?"

"If I knew I would tell you! He never got it out to me. He's going to tell me tomorrow or the next day."

"When did this happen?"

"Yesterday."

"I see. Has there been trouble at the Hall?"

"No," I said. Then I thought better of that. "Well, there has been, Dr. Strachey. One of the girls killed herself."

"Ah yes, the suicide," murmured Dr. Strachey. "Was this friend's conversation about that girl?"

"No. It was about other things that have been happening at the Hall."

"Other things?"

"Well, there are weird things going on."

"Things pertaining to—witchcraft—Aimee?"

Damn him! "Well, perhaps."

"Does your friend believe in witches, Aimee?"

"Yes."

"Do you believe in witches?"

"No!" I answered vehemently.

"You seem very sure of yourself," laughed Dr. Strachey.

"I am!"

"Agression is sometimes a sign of insecurity, Aimee," said Dr. Strachey in a mild voice.

"Whatever does that mean?"

"Your answer was quite aggressive," he told me. "I'd say offhand that you *wished* your answer was no; that perhaps you thought your *real* answer might be yes."

"Now we're getting back to that again!"

"Yes. Because it's the crux of the problem, it seems to me. Something to do with witches."

"Wait a minute. Are you talking about Salem again?"

"Yes. And the fact that you were afraid to visit the witch house."

"But I wasn't afraid—" I began. "Oh. I see what you mean."

"I mean simply that you were frightened to death not only of witches but of the very idea of witchcraft. I submit that you have always had a fear deep inside you that because you are descended from a family in which there was a possessed girl, you too might become possessed, or worse than that—might indeed be a witch yourself!"

I sat up and stared at Dr. Strachey, with a boiling sense of outrage rising in me.

"Relax, Aimee," he told me kindly. "We're just here to try to get at the truth."

"But if what you're saying is that I may be a witch—" I paused, unable to go on.

"My dear Mrs. Hammond, I am a doctor of psychiatry, and I have degrees in psychology, and a number of other sciences. Do I resemble the kind of man who would believe in witches? Are you quite daft? Of course I do not believe you are a witch, or capable of *being* a witch! I say that you might have *fears* of being a witch, that your own insecurity in regard to witchcraft has been making you believe that you might indeed be a witch, and that the blackouts, the lapses of memory, are all part of your psyche's attempt to block out such fears. Understand this, Mrs. Hammond, the psyche is the center of your self. The psyche does not involve itself in intellectual distinctions of any sort. It fears. It hates. It loves. And to protect the psyche, there are levels of conscious mind to prevent fears, horrors, and pain of all kinds from entry. It is your psyche that fears witchcraft, not the conscious you. But until we find out the *reason*, I am afraid we must accept the fact that it does fear; and that because it *does* fear, you too as an integrated being also fear witchcraft and the possibility of your own *possession*."

I stared at the ceiling.

"That's all, Mrs. Hammond. I'm afraid our time is up." He was very formal, suddenly.

Dr. Strachey had given me a great deal to think about, and I was so deeply involved in consideration of the events that had been going on around me for the past few weeks that I almost walked right past the Hall.

With the feeling of chagrin, I turned in at the old Colonial building, and walked up the stairs, glancing upward at the façade as I did, and thinking what a beautiful, old building it was for this day and age.

Then my eye roved across the front of the brick to the window of Mrs. Venefica's office, and I shuddered, remembering that that was the window from which Lora Blake had jumped to her death. And I saw the doormat and thought that beneath that, even now, lay the obscured form of the pentacle.

And I—who had always been so scientific and practical—now felt that, perhaps, I too had a superstitious dread of witchcraft, for Dr. Strachey had almost convinced me, in his short discussion of the psyche.

I wandered into the building and went to my office. For the moment, I had a great deal of work to do and I sat down and began fumbling at folders and papers. It must have been a half hour later when I got to the telephone call.

"Hello," I said. "Mrs. Hammond."

"Aimee," said a voice I knew quite well. "It's Ben."

"Hello, Ben!" I said, my voice brightening. "Believe it or not, you're cheering me up!"

He laughed. "Of course I am! Don't I always?"

"Not with your *spooky* face on!"

"Aimee, I've been working at the Town Hall all day. I've found out a great deal."

"About what, Ben?"

"About what's been going on at the Hall. And I want you to wait for me right there. I'm coming over with some very convincing proof."

I sat up straight. "Proof of what?"

"There is someone there practicing witchcraft," he said stoutly.

"Of course! Mrs. Venefica!"

"Perhaps. But it's a serious business. There is much

more to it than meets the eye. It has to do with demoniac possession—and with *death*!"

"All right, Ben," I said, smiling. "Ben. I've been talking to Dr. Strachey. He tells me I'm afraid of witchcraft because I have—I may have—oh—*tendencies*!"

There was a silence. "That's what I've been trying to tell you for months, now, Aimee."

"I know," I wailed, "but it isn't true!"

"Wait until you see what I've dug up, Aimee," Ben said in a strong voice. "Don't go anywhere. I'll be there in half an hour. I just want to finish what I'm on right now. I'm writing it all up. It's only a ten-minute walk."

"All right, Ben. I'll be waiting for you."

I smiled to myself and started in on the papers again.

It was three-thirty. I looked up. The office was very quiet. I had been simply sitting there, dreaming. No. I had not been dreaming. I had been looking at the papers in front of me. I had been working at the budget. But—

Three-thirty! I remembered the telephone call from Ben, and I wondered what time I had gotten the call. I had come back from Dr. Strachey's at two p.m., and had worked for fifteen minutes. Say two-fifteen. And Ben had said he would be over in half an hour. Two-forty-five. Then where was he? And where had that forty-five minutes between two-forty-five and three-thirty gone?

I stood up and opened the door at almost the same moment I heard the ambulance screaming up the street in front of the building and then turning the corner toward the center of town.

I ran outside.

There was a crowd gathering at the corner, and beginning to run across the street and over to the library.

Without thinking, I followed the crowd. I do not remember what I was thinking about at all, or *if* I was thinking. I seemed to be following instinct rather than reason.

The crowd was growing around a portion of the street near the Town Hall.

I looked across at the old stone building and saw white faces peering out of the dusty windows set in amidst the creeping ivy.

And then I found myself pushing through the crowd, trying to see who was lying on the pavement.

"He's gone," someone said near me.

I shoved and struggled and they let me through.

The blood was forming in a pool around his head. I could see the red hair and the tweed jacket that was so familiar and I knew without looking any closer at the torn and twisted body that the dead man was Ben Magruder.

"Hit and run," a woman said as I staggered back.

"Anybody get the number?" a policeman asked.

No one had.

I turned and looked directly into the plate glass window in front of Wagner's. I looked like a wraith of some kind—pale, almost transparent; sick; unbelieving.

PART THREE:
Bridget Bishop

Chapter Thirteen

Stunned and frightened, I sat at my desk, unable to force myself to go about my work. In my mind's eye I could still see that destroyed human body on the pavement in front of the Town Hall. I could see the torn jacket that I knew so well, the red hair matted with blood.

And as I sat there, unholy kind of intuition seized me.

I knew now exactly who had been behind all these strange happenings and the two deaths. I *knew*, and it was as if Ben Magruder were speaking to me from the beyond.

Consider:

Who would have lost the most if Lora Blake had lived to tell her story and point the finger at the one who had bedeviled her?

Who was the one person who could have pushed her out the window had she not chosen to jump out herself?

Who had heard the incantations on the fourth floor and had made a record of them and then destroyed it?

Who had pretended to befriend Lora Blake to help her escape and had then driven her back to the spot where Lora was in the most danger?

Who had known exactly where Ben Magruder would be in order to drive through the street at breakneck speed and run him down?

Who by heritage and by background was the person

most likely to be possessed by the devil and driven to madness and murder?

I sank back in the chair, unable to pursue the questioning any longer. Of course, it was true. There was only one person who answered all those points of identification.

Aimee Parris.

Yes!

I could hear Dr. Strachey questioning me again and again about my life in Salem. I could, once again, hear his discussion after I had failed to answer his questions. Yes. I was frightened of the witch house. Somehow, I believed that because I was a Parris and a possible direct descendent of Elizabeth Parris I had the proper heritage to become possessed once again three hundred years later.

Possession!

It was not the essential ability to be a witch that had driven me to my madness. It was the inbred memory of possession in 1692 that had returned to plague me now in the twentieth century.

That was what the nightmare signified, the nightmare and the memory lapses which had followed. And my wanton behavior with Don, too! What else was behind it but possession by evil spirits?

And then, when Ben Magruder had guessed the truth, but had been too decent to spell it out for me, I had totally ignored him, clinging to my pretense at rationality: that I did not believe in witches! I *thought* I did not believe in witches, just as Dr. Strachey had said. But apparently, I *did* believe in them in my own subconscious!

With Don I had acted like a spoiled child. When he had tried to get me to quit my job, I had flown into a rage and flatly refused. If I had listened to him, I would have quit! And Ben had tried to do the same thing that Don had failed to do—persuade me to quit at the Hall.

There was one reason I wanted and needed the Hall. Of course! I could see it clearly now. It was the presence of Mrs. Venefica, the woman who had turned herself deliberately into a witch in order to have something to do. I had chosen to stay at the Hall in order to hide my own activities under the obvious protection of Mrs. Venefica. If there *was* a witch at the Hall, if someone became possessed at the Hall, it would seem to be because of Mrs. Venefica—not because of Aimee Parris!

And when Lora Blake had become possessed, she did not know that I too was possessed, and had been possessed since I had come to the Hall! And I did not admit it to her because I did not really know it in my conscious mind. She had believed in me when I made that overt gesture to send her to California.

But I had taken her back to the Hall. I had handed her over to the evil that inhabited the Hall, the evil that possessed me and in turn possessed Lora Blake!

Everything fitted in. I had even run up to Mrs. Venefica's office when Lora Blake was struggling with Jill Towers—ostensibly to help Lora, but certainly to help kill her if she changed her mind or if Jill succeeded in saving her.

And once again, who had ignored Ben Magruder's telephone call from Town Hall? Who had erased the tape that I had made, when rational, and sent the erased tape to Ben? Aimee Parris, *possessed*!

I was shaking now with fear and abhorrence for myself.

I thought back. I remembered my memory lapse the afternoon after Ben had called. Yes. Obviously, I had gotten hold of someone's car and had driven down the deserted street to wait for Ben Magruder to start to cross in front of me and at that point I had driven the car right at him, hit him, and run over him.

Then I had returned to the Hall. Gradually, I had recovered my memory.

And I? Had I taken part in those covens? Or was I the *real* diabolist? The one who was really possessed? Perhaps I would never know.

And Mrs. Venefica? What about her? Was she really dying as Dr. Kingsley had told me? Or was she simply under the same spell I was? Or was she in reality *directing* me for—for *her* master?

I remembered Ben Magruder's original solution with interest: that Mrs. Venefica was old and dying and wanted a young body to inhabit. Was that true? Or was it something else? Was it perhaps the spirit that had inhabited the body of Elizabeth Parris in 1692—the spirit that wanted *my* body now?

I dreaded to think what might happen now that Ben Magruder was dead. The last person who had guessed the truth was out of the way. Now there would be no one to prevent complete possession of my body by the spirit that had already possessed me several times before.

It occurred to me that I should visit Mrs. Venefica on the fourth floor to find out how she might be feeling. The hallway was deserted when I went out and climbed the stairs slowly, still dazed and numb from Ben Magruder's death.

I rapped on the door, lightly at first. There was no answer. I rapped again and finally heard a hoarse voice from within: "Come in!"

I opened the door and stood inside the very close atmosphere of the room. There was not a breath of air stirring. The windows were all bolted tightly. It reminded me exactly of the way the room had felt the first time I had come inside it.

Mrs. Venefica lay in her bed in the far end of the office, her white face turned toward me.

"Hello, my dear," she said with a ghastly smile. "How are you?"

"Very well, Mrs. Venefica."

"You're not looking very well, Mrs. Hammond," she told me confidentially, squinting at me in the darkness of her room. "Have you been eating well?"

"I have just had a bad experience. A good friend of mine was killed in a hit-and-run accident."

"Oh, my poor child!" said Mrs. Venefica consolingly.

"Perhaps you know him, Ben Magruder."

She shook her head slowly. "I'm afraid I don't. Was he a resident of Coldwater?"

"Yes."

"Ben Magruder," said Mrs. Venefica thoughtfully.

"Mrs. Venefica," I said, suddenly losing all patience and deciding to drop all pretense. "Do you believe in witchcraft? I mean *really* believe in the Devil?"

Her eyes darted to my face and then a slow smile moved across her withered lips. "Not really, dear. It's a game, don't you know?"

"Do you believe in possession?"

She shook her head. "Of course there is no such thing. It is a myth."

"Can you cast a spell?"

"No, not really," she said softly. "Although I *pretend* I can."

"Then all your occult gifts are simply pretense?"

"No."

I stared. "Then what—?"

"I am clairvoyant."

I gaped. I knew that scientifically clairvoyance could be proven in a good percentage of cases.

"I am not trying to frighten you, Mrs. Hammond," she continued with a faint smile, "but I do sense *something* when I look at you."

"At me?"

"I sense disharmony, Mrs. Hammond. I sense fear and apprehension. And I sense discord and emotional unbalance."

I was about to interrupt her, but she went right on.

"There is more." She shut her eyes. "I see a house on a hill. There is a dark sky behind it. It is an old house—hundreds of years old. I see lightning striking in the clouds behind the house."

I said, "The house I live in is not old, Mrs. Venefica."

"I am not seeing your house. I am seeing a house in a remote part of the country, Mrs. Hammond. And I see you walking towards it."

"I?"

"The house has been the scene of great tragedy in the past. It has been a house of death. An inhabitant of the house hangs from the gallows. I cannot see who it is."

"Gallows?" I thought immediately of Salem.

"Now I see a name. Solemn. Salaam. Salem. Salem! That is the name. My dear, have you ever been in Salem?"

Her eyes penetrated mine.

"I was born there," I told Mrs. Venefica challengingly.

She blanched. Her eyes closed again. "I see you entering the house of death. You are visiting someone inside it. I do not see any more, Mrs. Hammond."

I shook my head. "I have never been in the witch house," I mused.

She looked at me piercingly. "You will be," she said. "Soon."

And that was all. Mrs. Venefica lay back, closed her eyes, and I walked out of the sick room confused and frightened.

Don took the death of Ben Magruder most calmly, considering that it was the death of someone he had known and loved. The very way his death had occurred was quick and merciful. I think that is why Don refused to worry too much about it. We had both known that Ben had a bad heart and had been sick recently. That he had died without a long period of suffering was a welcome thing, to us, actually.

"Darling, you're very quiet this evening," he told me later as we sat on our back porch in the dusk.

"Yes. Just a little headache. And Ben's sudden going like that . . ."

"I understand. Is there anything about the Hall that you'd like to discuss?"

"Not really," I said, dreading to think of what I had decided in the afternoon, and afraid to tell him what Mrs. Venefica had told me about the Salem witch house.

"You seem so quiet," he persisted.

"I'm just tired," I smiled. "Don't worry about me.

You don't think anything's going to happen to me at the Hall, now, do you?"

He laughed briefly. "I think I was overreacting. I'm sure there is nothing out of the way there. Ben was a very good convincer. But I never really believed."

"Good. Because I don't either. And I want to be able to relax and get into the job there."

"How is the old crone?"

"Mrs. Venefica?" I asked. "She's coming along."

"No more coven meetings?"

"No more," I said. "We've got her in bed."

"Keep her there," Don advised.

I nodded.

"And that's where we should be," Don said finally, reaching out and taking me by the hand.

It was hard to get to sleep. I kept thinking about Mrs. Venefica's vision. The few words she had used to describe the house convinced me that it was the witch house in Salem. The house had actually belonged to Goodwife and Goodman Procter. Someone had bought it years ago and preserved it. It had been moved from its original location, but it was visited even now as the "witch house." I had never been there, as I had told Dr. Strachey.

And if Mrs. Venefica had seen me entering it—and if she was not making up a vision—I would soon be going inside it! How could Mrs. Venefica make up the scene when she had not even known I was born in Salem?

Or had she known?

I thought again about Salem and about my parents and about Drew. I tossed and turned and got up once to try to tire myself out enough to fall asleep and noticed that the air had turned warm and sticky. Then, before I could get back in the bedroom, lightning struck nearby and it began to rain hard.

I got into bed but the sound of the thunder and the splashing of the rain on the sides of the house and the roof kept me tossing and turning without being able to doze off.

And then, suddenly, I did drop off.

Lightning flashed. Heat blazed about me. Brilliant, blue light illuminated the bedroom. I was standing in the middle of the floor now, staring down at the bed in which Don slept.

My hair was soaked with perspiration, and it hung down about my neck and shoulders. I was in my thin nightgown, shaking with anxiety and fear.

I turned to stare about me, but I could see nothing. The lightning flash had momentarily blinded me. I wondered what I was doing out of bed, standing there in the middle of the floor.

I realized to my horror at that point that I was holding something in my hand—my right hand. I looked down. The dull flash of metal showed in my hand.

With my left hand I touched the object gingerly. I recoiled. It was a long kitchen knife—the one with the serrated blade that I used to cut bread!

Before I could react another flash of lightning caught me poised there frozen in an attitude of potential threat.

I was leaning over Don, holding the knife, about to plunge it into his throat!

Sobbing, I straightened, and moved back, letting the knife clatter to the floor.

Don stirred in bed, turned over, and opened his eyes.

"Darling," he muttered.

"Here I am!" I said, moving quickly toward him, the perspiration pouring off my body.

He held me and sat up in bed. "What are you doing out of bed?"

I glanced at the floor where the long knife still lay. "I—I was frightened of the lightning, dear."

"Oh," he said, and grinned. "Don't be afraid. Come on back to bed."

I said, "I want to wash my face."

He looked at me and then lay back. After a moment, he turned over and closed his eyes. Then I stooped over and picked up the knife, which I carried with me into the kitchen.

When I got there I saw that the silver drawer was open, as if I had come in and flung it out in a hurry to get the knife.

Whatever the evil forces in the Hall, they had most certainly entered me and were now controlling my every move. What else but evil could have caused me to walk in my sleep, grab up a knife, and stand poised at the edge of Don's bed, about to plunge it into his throat?

Chapter Fourteen

It was as if I had been standing there in the lobby of the Hall for a very long time. For the life of me I could not remember anything that had happened that morning. I glanced at my wrist watch. It was ten-thirty. Through the front doors I could see the sunshine and the street outside.

I tried to think my way back step by step to breakfast, but my memory was hopelessly confused. I simply could not remember one thing that had happened to me that morning. I could not even remember the ride down in the car with Don.

Don . . .

My memory raced backwards then, across the void of forgetfulness, and centered on that startling instant in the early morning as I had stood in the center of my bedroom, a knife in my hand, and Don lying there peacefully and helpless in sleep.

I felt myself shaking with fear.

What had happened after that? I put the knife away, and then I came back to bed. I crawled in under the covers ...

To save my soul I could not *remember* crawling in under the covers. I was only imagining that I had crawled under the covers. There is no way that I could actually *remember* going back to bed.

What had I done?

Where had I gone?

And Don—where was he?

Common sense assured me that Don was right where he always was—in his office in New York City.

And if I telephoned him in a panic, he would really wonder what had happened to me and begin urging me again to get away from the Hall.

I did not want to go through that just yet.

My appointment with Dr. Strachey was at one o'clock.

I had some difficulty telling him about my experience of the night before, but he was patient and soon I got it all out.

"I was standing there, the knife in my hand, poised to plunge it in his throat," I said, appalled at the melodrama in my voice.

"I see," said Dr. Strachey calmly.

"I screamed and dropped the knife. He woke up."

"Was he frightened?"

"No. He did not even know I had held the knife. I waited until he turned over to go back to sleep, and put it back."

He made notes. "And then?"

"Then—" I opened my eyes and stared at the ceiling. "I don't *know*!"

"Academic," said Dr. Strachey with satisfaction.

"Academic?" I repeated. "I try to kill my husband. I lose my memory. That's academic?"

"Of course," said Dr. Strachey in that maddeningly casual way of his. "Don't you see the pattern yet?"

I did not, and I told him I did not.

He sighed. "All right, Aimee. Let's go back to the

148

beginning, shall we? It's all come clear now, and it should be no problem at all to stop the nightmares and the lapses of memory."

"I'm glad to hear it," I rejoined sarcastically.

"The very selection of a knife has a most significant meaning, don't you see?"

"I do not see," I maintained stubbornly.

"Well, if you had selected a gun, I doubt that it would *mean* the same thing. Or if you had chosen to poison him—no, no." Dr. Strachey broke off his musing and sighed.

"What does the knife mean?" I asked in exasperation.

"Well of course if you think about it, it becomes obvious." He looked over the edge of the couch at me suggestively.

"I don't know!" I told him.

"Well, castration, of course."

Castration! I stared in dismay.

"Symbolic castration," said Dr. Strachey, warming up to the subject. "Your whole history is one of repression of sexual urges, Aimee. It's almost as if you're a direct descendent of those early New England Puritans who pretended that sex did not exist except as something the Devil controlled."

"But I'm *not* repressed," I said to him.

"Maybe not physically, but in your mind you have definite sex repressions," he said. "Think back to your home town. You were engaged to a young man named Drew. But the engagement was broken up by your parents, because Drew was *too male* for you."

I glared at him. "That's not true!"

"Ultimately, it is, Aimee. You bowed to your parents' wishes. You gave up the man you loved for them, because you thought they were right, that you were in love with him physically and not spiritually."

My mouth must have been hanging open.

"Then you escaped and married, and obviously have had a fairly normal sex life with your husband."

"Very normal!" I snapped.

"On the surface, perhaps!" Dr. Strachey retorted. "But underneath, there is something else at work."

"What?" I was getting annoyed at him.

"Your background and upbringing has made you one thing, Aimee, but your emergence into the sophisticated world outside of that narrow-minded, little town in which you grew up has made you want to change into something else. There is a conflict inside you. On the one hand, your narrow-minded upbringing wants you to be a Puritan maiden, even throughout marriage. On the other hand, your knowledge of life and your, obviously normal, physical needs have shaped you into another person, almost the opposite of the Puritan maiden. The lusty side of you, if you will permit me to categorize it as such, is at war with the puritanical side."

"But so far—"

"Nothing has happened?" Dr. Strachey lifted an eyebrow. "What about the nightmare? The burning nightmare?"

I shook my head. "Nothing important," I said.

"On the contrary. It is a most important manifestation of the inner conflict within you."

"How so?"

"You will recall that during the first nightmare you changed into something else you never had been. Your husband attested to that, if I am not mistaken."

I flushed. "It is only a coincidence."

"No, Aimee. It is *proof* of what I am saying. The nightmare, and the memory lapse, is all a smoke screen to provide your id, the inner core of you, the opportunity to be what it wants to be. While your conscious mind screens out your acts, your id takes over your personality, you do what you want to do with your husband, and you become warm and loving and uninhibitedly affectionate."

I was dumbstruck.

"And that is what all this is about, Aimee. Your two halves have been fighting one another for some years. Now your conscious mind has given up the fight and has let your unconscious self take over at periods when the conscious mind absents itself. For conscious mind, read Puritan conscience. You can love your husband with as much abandonment as you wish, and your conscience will never know!"

"But—"

"The scene last night is simply the latest playing out of the conflict. The conflict is not resolved. One part of you wants to be lusty and abandoned, and the other wants to be prim and restricted. Last night, your puritanical side took over, and brought the knife from the kitchen into the bedroom. As I said before, for the purpose of symbolic castration, so that your 'other' self would never have the urge again to become wanted."

"Absolute balderdash!" I snorted. "What about the time I thought I took Lora Blake to the airport?"

Dr. Strachey leaned back. "That is just a bit more complicated. The problem there was slightly different. You had just had a quarrel with your husband. Right? And you had disobeyed him out of spite and gone off with the girl from the Hall. Right?"

"Yes."

"You were trying to get back at Don for being so overbearing. And at the same time you wanted to make up with him, intimately. Ambivalence, Aimee. You desired opposites, simultaneously. Therefore, you simply pretended to drive the girl to the airport, turned around, deposited her at the Hall, and came home to make love to Don."

"Nonsense!" I snorted. Yet, how did I know that Dr. Strachey had told the truth? I would simply have to ask Don about that.

"But what about the tape recorder?"

"Much more complicated," said Dr. Strachey. "Here we have a situation in which your own mind is not at rest. Besides your inner conflict—the earthy against the spiritual side of you, let's say—you also have a conflict about witchcraft. You do not know whether you believe or disbelieve in witches! I have said you really do believe in witches, but have been afraid to admit it to yourself. If you will accept that supposition—"

"For the moment," I agreed.

"The tapes are proof that Ben Magruder is right. Someone *is* practicing witchcraft at the Hall. Your conscious mind fights the truth. You do not want to admit that Ben is right. You simply erase the tape and send it out to him blank so he will not be able to have the proof himself. And then you quite conveniently forget what you have done!"

"What about my failure to go to the Town Hall to meet him?"

"Exactly the same thing. You *knew* he had proof. You did not want to face the fact."

"But Dr. Strachey, you have said time and time again that *you* do not believe in witches or witchcraft. Why then are you saying that my own mind was unsure? Is yours *sure*? I mean, how can one half of me believe and the other half not believe?"

"That is your problem, Aimee—not mine!" smiled Dr. Strachey. "Once you resolve the conflict, then you will not be subject to memory lapses and other such phenomenon."

"Then the memory lapse because of my conflict over witchcraft is quite different from the memory lapse because of my conflict over lust and repression?"

"Yes," nodded Dr. Strachey.

"But how can you account for the dissimilarity of motivation and the similarity of symptoms?"

"Aimee, once the human mind discovers a method of protecting its inner secrets, it will use the same method to protect any manner of different kinds of secrets!"

"But what am I going to do about last night? How am I going to find out what happened between the time I put the knife away and the time I regained my memory back in the Hall?"

"I'd suggest you telephone your husband and find out," Dr. Strachey said mildly.

"And now, what about my next appointment? Or am I through with my therapy?"

He shook his head. "Absolutely not. Simply knowing what is at the root of your problem, and making the nightmare and the memory lapses vanish are two very different things. I'll see you again at the usual time."

I sat in my office and dialed long distance. The switchboard at Don's office answered.

"I'd like to speak to Don Hammond, please."

"Who is calling?" a girl asked in a sing-song voice.

"Mrs. Hammond."

"I'll connect you."

There was a fairly long pause. Then someone picked up the telephone. "Hello? Mr. Hammond's wire."

"May speak to Mr. Hammond," I said.

"Mr. Hammond is not in. Who is calling, please?"

"His wife," I said. "Where has he gone?"

There was a brief pause. "I really don't know," the voice said. "Mrs. Hammond, this is Jean Rice. We've spoken before."

"Oh, yes, Jean. Where has he gone?"

"I thought you might know that better than I. We called the house, of course, but no one was in. I'm afraid I don't have the number of your business phone."

"But—" I choked. "Isn't Don *there*?"

"No, ma'am. As I said—"

"I mean, didn't he come in this morning?"

"No, he didn't. We tried to telephone the house to find out what had delayed him, or if he was sick or something, but we couldn't reach anyone."

"No," I said weakly. "Of course not."

"Do you know where he is, Mrs. Hammond?"

I stared at the phone. "I really don't, Jean. But as soon as I find out, I'll let you know."

"Thank you, Mrs. Hammond." I knew by the sound of her voice that she was terribly embarrassed for me.

I hung up, my thoughts in a whirl. It was easy to rationalize their reaction at Don's office. Most of them would think that there was some quarrel between the two of us, and that Don had gone somewhere to cool off.

But I knew that there had been no quarrel. Only that

153

momentary instant of horror when I had come to, holding that knife poised at his throat.

And then—blankness.

What had happened after I put the knife away?

Had I once again risen, assuming I had gone to bed, gotten the knife, and carried out my original intention?

Had I killed my husband?

Was he at home right now—dead in bed—amidst . . . ?

The car was not in the driveway, nor was it in the garage. I ran from the cab and pulled out my key. It would not fit in the lock, and I struggled with it for a few mad moments before it went in and the door opened inward.

I ran through the living room and into the bedroom.

The beds were made.

I stared at the bed, then pulled it apart and examined it carefully.

Nothing.

No blood. No traces of violence.

Yet I had read of murderers who had carefully cleaned up after their crimes and had left the site of homicide spic and span.

Don. Where was he? Had I taken him somewhere—and—abandoned him—in our car perhaps?

I was shaking as I came out of the house and stood looking at the taxicab in the street.

Don! I cried out to myself.

As I was standing there, something made me turn around and look into the living room. It was just as I had last seen it the night before except for one thing.

On the little table near the front door, there was a piece of paper—typewriter size—lying open. It looked like it had been torn out of an envelope hastily and then left there.

I walked across to pick it up.

A note from Don?

No.

I read:

"Dearest Don. All the excitement at the Hall and

Ben Magruder's sudden death has tired me terribly. I don't want to worry you or to take you away from important work at the office.

"I'm going to Mother's for a day or two. Don't worry. You can always call me there tonight. Please forgive me for making up my mind without consulting you. Believe me, it's for the best.

"I'll be taking the train.

Aimee."

I let the paper flutter away from me and stared into space.

Then, immediately, I let out a whoop of delight. I ran for the telephone and put in an immediate long distance call to my home in Massachusetts.

In a moment I was speaking with Mother.

"Goodness!" she was saying, obviously to my father. "It's Aimee! How are you, Aimee?"

"Pretty good, Mom. Listen. It's a long and tangled story, but has Don come up there to Salem?"

"Don? No. He hasn't. Is something wrong, Aimee?"

"No. Please don't worry." My heart sank. "I just thought he might have come up there. Did he call you?"

"No," said my mother slowly. "Did you think he had? What's going on there, Aimee?"

"Nothing, Mother," I said impatiently. "I'm sorry I bothered you."

"If he calls, I'll tell him to call *you*. Is that right, Aimee?"

"I guess so," I said weakly. "Give my best to Father. I'll call you later and talk longer."

I hung up, distraught.

I saw now that the note I had written might well be a false trail. In other words, I might have written the note to mislead the police if they began looking for Don.

If I had killed him, that is.

Chapter Fifteen

I fumbled in my bag for money to pay the cab driver and saw the key that Ben Magruder had given me some days ago.

"I've changed my mind," I told the driver, and got back in the cab. I gave him Ben Magruder's address in the Ridges.

The driver found the place with little trouble.

I paid him and got out, waiting until he had driven off through the dense woods before turning and walking up the pathway to the front door of the small cottage.

It was a clapboard house, some fifty years old, built very small. The magnificent woods around it fully screened it off from every other house nearby. Most of the neighboring houses were large rambling ones. This cottage could have been the house of a caretaker engaged in tending the grounds of one of the nearby estates.

The afternoon sun came through the leaves, making flashes of light on the outside of the little white house.

I inserted the key and the door sprang open.

It was just as I remembered it the last time Don and I had come to see Ben. I closed the door behind me and looked around. Ben had his desk in the far corner of the room, crammed with papers and covered with books and folders.

I have no idea what I was looking for—if anything. It was simply that the sight of the key had brought my mind back to Ben. Suddenly, I wanted to talk to him. Since Ben was dead, the best way to talk to him was to visit his house and look through his papers. He had worked very hard on those papers, and had been working on them when he met his death.

Had I caused that death?

If Dr. Strachey was right, I had certainly *not* caused his death.

If Ben was right, perhaps I had.

I sat down at his desk and began reading the top papers of those spread out before me. They contained notes scrawled in Ben's large, rambling hand. I could make out the words plainly.

It was his grocery list.

I pushed aside the sheet and looked at another.

"Venefica," it said. Then below it there was another name. "Sarah Welch." There was an address in Coldwater. Then a note: "Teacher. 31 years. Coldwater School System. Mill River Grammar. Central Grammar." Then, farther down on the sheet, there was another notation: "Fairfield Mental Home, 1961 through 1969. Discharged."

So Mrs. Venefica had been a mental case, and her name was really Sarah Welch.

I read further.

"Forced to resign from teaching staff of Mill River Grammar School. Accused by P.T.A. mothers of stressing the occult in her classroom. No proof, but S. Welch was accused of running a witch coven in the school. Accuser was later given psychiatric treatment for hysteria. Other teachers simply granted that S. Welch was a 'bit of a screwball.' But she apparently did practice witchcraft, even though only in fun."

The last phrase was underlined in Ben Magruder's heavy hand.

I could hear Ben speaking now:

"It is not the fact of witchcraft you have to fear. It is the fact that *someone believes* in witchcraft. If one person believes in demonology, it works."

According to Ben, Mrs. Venefica, who had changed her name from "Welch" to "Witch", believed in witchcraft and practiced witchcraft. And because of that she had been dismissed from Mill River Grammar School and was later forced to spend several years in the Fairfield Mental Home.

And she was dying, according to Dr. Kingsley.

Was she trying to bewitch me? Possess my body? Live on in me? I felt the chill wind of fear hovering over me, remembering Ben's strange explanation of the memory lapses I had been suffering and of my burning nightmare.

My hand shook. I glanced around. Was there someone watching me here in this supposedly deserted cottage? I saw the breeze move the curtains. Or was it the breeze? Was it Ben's spirit hovering there, trying to communicate with me?

I sighed, and stirred the pages again.

And I found the list.

My name led the list. That is, part of my name. Parris.

The list ran: Elizabeth Parris.

Abigail Williams.

Those two girls were the first to be "possessed" by spirits in the household of Reverend Samuel Parris in Salem Village, 1692.

I looked on down the list. The names seemed vaguely familiar, possibly from some reading I had done in the long ago past.

Mary Walcott.

Elizabeth Booth.

Susanna Sheldon.

Elizabeth Hubbard.

Sarah Churchill.

Mary Warren.

Ann Putnam.

I remembered. They were the names of the most vociferous of the "possessed" girls in Salem. They were those who had been drawn into witchcraft by practicing it with Tituba, the Caribbean Indian slave of the Parris household.

Under this list Ben Magruder had written:

"They practiced witchcraft."

I lifted the page.

More names.

Rebecca Nurse.
Sarah Good.
Elizabeth How.
Sarah Wild.
Susanna Martin.
Bridget Bishop.
Elizabeth Proctor.
John Willard.
George Jacobs.
Martha Carrier.
George Burroughs.
John Proctor.

And more. Underneath this list Ben had written: "Hanged as witches, 1692."

I wondered why Ben had been writing down these names. For some reason he seemed to have developed a one-track mind with regard to the Salem witchcraft trials. What could they have to do with me—or with the current trouble at the Hall?

I was afraid that poor Ben had become a fanatic about Salem and had lost his reason.

I shifted the sheets once again and this time I noticed a peculiar thing. As I picked up the sheet I held it slightly askew to the light. The rays of the sun coming in through the half-open window showed a small indentation in the paper. It resembled an X. But the X had been erased carefully.

I stared at the sheet.

It was the page listing the names of the "possessed" girls—the accusers.

The name closest to the X, which was in the margin, was Mary Warren.

It did not make any sense to me.

What puzzled me was the fact that the X had been erased. Ben Magruder must have erased it. Why had he not simply run a pencil mark through the name if it was in error?

Why erase the X?

That was not like Ben.

I started going through the rest of the sheets and came to a strange drawing that I could not at first identify. Then I could see that it resembled a crude kind of child's doll—a piece of rag with bristles sticking out of the top, like hair. Eyes and nose and mouth were drawn in on the face, and the rest of the cloth was twisted and tied to resemble arms, legs, and a crude body.

At the bottom of the drawing Ben had written: "Poppet."

I closed my eyes. I could remember the term somewhere. Where? What did "poppet" mean?

I looked at the rest of Ben's scrawl.

"Earlier version of 'puppet.' From Middle English, 'popet.' Apparently derived from Middle Low German *poppe*, 'doll.' From lower Latin *puppa*, variation of Latin *pupa, 'doll.'* "

Poppet! My eyes widened. I knew what the poppet was used for. Witches practicing witchcraft in Salem had used the poppet to put spells on other girls!

The idea was to stick a pin in the poppet of Jane, for instance, and make Jane experience a headache, arm ache, or stomachache.

Silly.

Ben had laboriously transcribed the writing and had tried to draw one of the New England poppets from the Salem witchcraft days.

I turned the sheet.

"Counter-sorcery," he had labeled the next page.

"If the accursed knows who is putting the curse on him, he need only find the medium of the curse—a potion, a poppet, an object—and reverse the curse by putting the curser's name on the poppet and modifying the poppet to conform to the physical characteristics of the curser."

I stared at that a long time, and then shook my head. Certainly Ben Magruder had been carried away by this witchcraft thing! To believe in such a simple and superstitious thing as a voodoo doll!

I remembered again Ben's statement: If one person believes in voodoo, it works.

I lifted the sheet and saw a Xeroxed copy of a birth certificate.

"Lora Blake," Ben Magruder had written at the top

of the page. Further on down, the name "Lora Lee Blake" was written in on the form, with the certificate signed by an official in King County, Illinois. I remembered that Lora Blake had come from some town in Illinois. Why had Ben Magruder sent away for this birth certificate?

I turned the page.

Now I saw a Xeroxed copy of a marriage license. It was dated some thirty years ago, and attested to the fact that Emily Ann Warren had married John William Blake in King County, Illinois. There was a date written in, and the marriage license was duly signed by the county clerk.

I puzzled over that for a moment, and then went on to the next sheet, to find out what other information about Lora Blake had been included in Ben's papers.

The next sheet contained more names. I turned back and puzzled over the marriage certificate once again. I did not really understand why Ben had included it in the sheaf of papers. I could see that he was trying to tie up Lora's death with witchcraft—with Mrs. Venefica, quite possibly. I tried to remember her real name. Ah! Sarah Welch! So?

I looked back at the birth certificate but could find nothing that looked familiar. I continued leafing through the sheets under the marriage license.

More names.

Willa Gayle.

Ellen Putnam.

Aimee Parris (Hammond).

Lora Blake.

Jill Towers.

Doreen Gray.

Sandy Mason.

Lenore Ulrich.

June Moore.

Patience Thompson.

Mary Leland.

Beside the name Willa Gayle, Ben had scrawled another name Will(iams)a (Abi)Gayle.

And the name Putnam had been circled. So had my

maiden name, Parris. There was a question mark after Lora Blake's name. But none of the other names was touched.

Will(iams)a (Abi)Gayle. Certainly! Reverse that and you had (Abi)Gayle Will(iams)a. Abigail Williams!

And if you took the Putnam from Ellen Putnam, and added a name, you might have Ann Putnam.

And Parris—

Yes! I saw the reason those names led the list. Williams, Putnam, and Parris appeared on *two* lists. This last list, and the first list—the list of accusers in Salem. I could see the logic in that.

But why was Lora's name questioned? And why had that other name "Mary Warren" been Xeroxed on the other sheet?

And then erased?

Suddenly, it occurred to me that Gayle Williams, Ellen Putnam, and Lora Blake were all dead! Of the four, I was the only one alive!

Warren! Then I remembered something, and pawed back through the sheets.

No. I had lost it.

I shuffled the pages again, and then the Xeroxed sheet of the marriage certificate fell out.

My eyes caught the name of her mother. Emily Ann Warren.

Warren.

Emily Warren. *Mary Warren.*

Willa Gayle. *Abigail Williams.*

Ellen Putnam. *Mary Putnam.*

Aimee Parris. *Elizabeth Parris.*

Pairs!

And of the four in the first list, three were dead! Lora Blake—whose mother had been a Warren! Willa Gayle—whose name was an anagram of Abigail Williams! Ellen Putnam—whose family name was Putnam!

Yes! Four possible descendents of the Salem accusers—and three of them were dead!

Who was trying to kill off the descendents of the accusers? Who but a witch who had been hanged on the gallows on their word? Who but someone bent on exacting vengeance for a 1692 wrong? Who but a witch whose soul lived on today in another body and hated those girls?

Who but—I pawed for the sheet of paper.

Rebecca Nurse. Sarah Good. Elizabeth How. Sarah Wild. Susanna Martin. Bridget Bishop. And more.

It was so simple as it sat there staring me in the face! Of course Ben Magruder had been excited. He had discovered a possible motive for three deaths—Willa Gayle, Ellen Putnam, and Lora Blake. And he had discovered a possible motive for my own series of mental lapses and that nightmare of burning.

I *was* next—as he had warned me. As he had warned me before he too was killed!

I sat back from my work and stared around me. There were two books lying on the floor near the desk. They were both about the Salem trials. I picked them up and started to leaf through one.

"Even as much as labor was needed in the colony, people had long ago developed a reluctance to incur the presence of Sarah Good in their homes, for she could be shrewish, idle, and above all slovenly. During the late epidemic she had been accused of spreading smallpox, if not by malefaction, at least by negligence. She had lately become something of a tramp, begging from door to door, being often not only rebuffed but followed to see that she did not bed down in the haymow and set the place afire with her evil-smelling pipe . . ."

". . . On Tuesday, July 19, the five were hanged on Gallows Hill, all women, the five whose trials had begun late in June: Rebecca Nurse, Goody Good, Elizabeth How, Sarah Wild, Susanna Martin. The ceremony was carried out with only one discordant note. When Reverend Noyes made one last appeal to Sarah Good to save her immortal soul by confessing that she was a witch, she answered:

" 'You're a liar! I am no more a witch than you are a wizard! If you take my life away, God will give you blood to drink.'

"And Noyes did have blood to drink, twenty-five years later, when he lay dying of a hemorrhage . . ."

Vengeance! If Sarah Good's word on her death was prophetic, it meant she *could* come back to earth years later and exact vengeance. Perhaps her spirit was still able to work evil on the living!

". . . The first of the Salem witches to be tried was Bridget Bishop. There was little occasion to prove witchcraft, this being evident and notorious to all beholders. Thanks to her flashy taste in dress—she frequently wore a red, paragon bodice—her smooth and flattering manner with men, the questionable gaieties that had gone on in the two taverns she owned, she had been gossiped about as a witch as far back as King Philip's War.

"She was the village Circe, dressed in red and excess lace to entrance the menfolk. Her house, past and present, had been ransacked, and the searchers had found in the cellar of the old house in Salem Village poppets made of rags and hog's bristles, stuck with headless pins . . .

"On June 10, High Sheriff George Corwin took her to the top of Gallows Hill and hanged her from the branches of a great oak tree . . ."

Poppets and pins! I thought. Here was a *real* witch! And she would be able to return to take vengeance on those who had hanged her on Gallows Hill in 1692!

I shivered and gathered together the papers and the books and took them with me when I left Ben Magruder's house. I wanted to get back to the Hall to talk to Mrs. Venefica. There was still something about her . . .

I telephoned for a cab, waited, and finally was driven back to the Hall. It was quite dark when I entered the building. Mrs. Grant had gone home. The girls were upstairs, and the bottom floor was deserted. I put the papers in my desk and locked the drawer. Then I mounted the stairs and knocked on Mrs. Venefica's office door.

There was no answer.

I tried to open it, found the door unlocked, and

pushed my way in. The little office was dark. I snapped on the lights. The moment I saw the condition of the sick bed I pressed back against the wall in shock.

It was Mrs. Venefica. She had tumbled half out of bed, and lay there wrapped in her bedclothes, her head hanging down, her tongue out of her mouth. Her face was congested.

I quickly lifted her and put her back in the bed. Checking her pulse, I found it to be faint indeed. She seemed to be in a coma. I checked her skin—it was pale. She was breathing shallowly, and seemed more dead than alive. In seconds, I was on the phone with Dr. Kingsley.

"It's Mrs. Venefica," I told him, as soon as I had identified myself.

"What's happened?"

"She seems to be in a coma."

"I'll be right over."

I waited for him, and simply because of the *vibrations* in the Hall, the news traveled like wildfire, and one by one the girls came in to look at her and to speak to me briefly.

At last Dr. Kingsley came. He made me leave the little office, and examined Mrs. Venefica in private. In a moment he stuck his head out through the open door.

"We're taking her to the hospital. It's a heart attack. It looks very serious."

I dialed for him and he called the hospital for an ambulance.

Soon the banshee wail of the siren curled through the town of Coldwater, the attendants came huffing and puffing up the stairs, carried Mrs. Venefica down and tucked her into the back of the ambulance, then set off in the direction of Coldwater Hospital with the siren going again.

I drove after them with Dr. Kingsley.

"Does Mrs. Grant know?" he asked me.

I admitted to him that I had forgotten to call her, and assured him I would tell her as soon as we got to the hospital.

Once at the hospital, I accompanied him up the

stairs to the Intensive Care Unit where they took Mrs. Venefica. It was crowded with machinery of all kinds, the white-faced dials gleaming dully in the light. I do not know exactly what they did to her, but they tried to bring her back to life.

Dr. Kingsley sat outside with me, waiting.

My mind wandered about, not only over the notes I had read in Ben Magruder's hand, but over my own lapses of memory and the strange things that had been happening to me ever since I had begun working at Fairfield Residence Hall.

Mostly, I thought about Ben's thesis that some witch was trying to insinuate her spirit into my body and push mine out. And I realized that if Ben's promise were true Mrs. Venefica's spirit at this point would be doing all it could to gain possession of my body.

With an embarrassment that made me very self-conscious, I fought against the entry of any other will into my mind, thinking myself foolish as I did so, yet I continued to concentrate on retaining my reason and my memory through all the moments I sat there.

There seemed to be no attempt to "take over" my body—whatever that could mean. I had moments of amusement when the whole game struck me as stupid and silly, but I continued my "vigil" because I remembered how even though Ben Magruder's ideas had struck me as so strange that I had laughed at him at first, later he was proved right.

I willed myself to allow no outside force to enter and . . .

In thirty minutes it was all over.

"She's gone," said a large, hulking, blond-haired man whom Dr. Kingsley addressed as Dr. Knightsbridge.

"There was not much that could be done, Mrs. Hammond," Dr. Kingsley told me.

I nodded, stunned at the abruptness of the attack and its aftermath.

Because, of course, now I had no suspect at all. *No one but myself!* I had hoped that Mrs. Venefica could answer some most interesting questions that had come up as I studied Ben Magruder's papers.

Now I could ask no one but myself.

"Thank you, Dr. Kingsley," I said numbly.

He drove me home and I went inside. It had slipped my memory that Don was not there, and I simply unlocked the door and went inside without thinking.

I turned on the light and sat on the couch exhausted. I was hungry, but too tired right at that moment to cook myself dinner. And Don . . .

Then it poured back into my memory. *Don had gone!*

The chances were very good that I had driven him away, or that I had even killed him . . .

The notes in Ben Magruder's cottage, however, seemed to proclaim my innocence. If the ancient curse of vengeance made by the condemned and hanged witches was indeed being carried out, then my name was on the death list with Lora Blake's because we were direct or indirect lineal descendants of the original accusers in the Salem witch trials. And the actual murderer of Lora Blake would be on the list of witches hanged at Salem on the gallows at Gallows Hill. Now that Mrs. Venefica had died without trying to exact vengeance from me, it meant that she had *not* killed Lora Blake.

I was thoroughly confused.

There was logic there, but it was most perplexing. Something about Mrs. Venefica's death seemed to distort the whole picture, throw it out of focus.

I wandered into the kitchen and then out onto the darkened back porch where it was peaceful and quiet. I sank down into the chair without turning on the light and closed my eyes, listening to the night sounds.

Witches. Curses. Suicides. I shuddered.

Then I felt cold hands on my throat. *Real, live, cold human hands!* Strangling me? I could not be sure.

I screamed and fell into a dead faint.

Chapter Sixteen

Don's eyes were big with concern.

"Aimee! What happened? What's the matter with you?"

He was leaning over me, patting my face with a cold towel. He had carried me into the living room, where the lights were blazing. I could only lie there numbly and stare at him in shock.

"Aimee! Where have you been? I've been worried sick—"

"*You've* been worried sick!" I retorted, finally getting my voice back, along with my anger. "Where have *you* been?"

Don frowned. "But I got your note this morning and I drove up to Salem to bring you back!"

"Why? Why didn't you call to tell me?"

"Honey! You weren't around at all! I got up and you'd left a note saying you were taking the train. I called the station, and the train had left. I was frantic! About that time the special delivery letter came and—"

"What special delivery letter?"

"That's the reason I drove up to Salem to find you. It's a paper from Ben Magruder, obviously written just before he was killed. The police, or someone, found it near the body, and sent it on to you, because it was written to you. It tells everything!"

"Tells everything?" I repeated faintly. Did it tell who was trying to kill me? I wondered.

"I'll get it," Don said. "You read it."

"But I called Mother at home, and you weren't there."

"I never got there," said Don. "The transmission went out in Hartford and I had to spend the rest of the day having it fixed. By evening I decided that I had better come back, and I called to tell you. Your mother told me you had changed your mind and were home. But there was no one home. I simply drove back and got here a half hour ago. But you were gone somewhere. I called the Hall, but no one knew where you were. There was a lot of excitement about Mrs. Venefica. And so I went out on the porch to wait for you and fell asleep. I woke up when you came in."

I stared up at my husband, and his face was guileless and untroubled. And after all I had been through that ghastly day—thinking I might have killed him, thinking I had buried his body somewhere, thinking he was dead!

"Darn you!" I snapped. "Why do you always have to be right! Now let me see that thing Ben sent!"

Don brought back a manila envelope and pulled out a few sheets of paper.

He was smiling at me.

"Dearest Aimee," I read aloud.

"It's time to stop the charade. Things have gotten a bit out of hand. Even natural events are beginning to look sinister to you, now that you have been swept up in the unreality of it. I did not know things would go so far when I started out my little experiment."

I looked up at Don, frowning.

"Read on," he said with a satisfied smile.

I did. "I told you once, Aimee, that belief is essential to the success of witchcraft. If you believe in witchcraft, that makes witchcraft a fact. If you believe in voodoo, that makes voodoo a fact. I still subscribe to that opinion. I have to. It is true.

"You scoffed at my statement. You said that witchcraft was *not* a fact even if it was believed.

"And that was what angered me so much that I had to show you the truth by a scientific method.

"Essentially, what I did was this:

169

"I *made* you dream your nightmares. I *made* you have your memory lapses. I *made* you believe that Mrs. Venefica was a witch. I *made* you believe that Lora Blake killed herself because she was possessed. I even *made* you suspect that you had killed her.

"Confess it, Aimee! Did you not believe that at one point?

"It was relatively easy. I did not even have to confide in Don. I simply worked on your subconscious. You remember the time I came over to talk to you? We had coffee. I drugged your cup, Aimee, and I subjected you to hypnotism. And your memory lapses came about because of *post-hypnotic* suggestion I instilled in you then.

"And because I was *suggesting* it to you, you began to believe that you yourself might be possessed by the devil's spirit. Am I right? You, a total disbeliever. You, a rational being. You, a most sensible girl! I had you believing that you might yourself be possessed!"

I looked up from the sheet of paper, the typed letters blurring in front of my eyes.

"Don!" I whispered weakly. "I can't believe it!"

He grinned. "Read on, Aimee."

"It all went wrong when that dreadful situation with Lora Blake occurred. It was a horrible coincidence, actually, but once it had happened, of course, it even suited my purposes more admirably. Because I wanted you to *believe* and then I wanted to be able to jolt you out of belief by telling you the truth—that you had been *tricked* into believing! And that was my thesis.

"But it was becoming too serious, and Don was worrying. I tried to calm him down, so that he would not ruin everything. And of course I made your periods of lapsed memory grow longer and longer—by the simple use of drugs and post-hypnotic suggestion.

"Don's stories about the garroting and the suicide bolstered up my theory admirably. I used them to the hilt, my dear. I confess that it snowballed once it had started. And then I saw you becoming more and more desperate. When Lora Blake came to you and wanted help, and you simply could not help her, but drove her back to the Hall, I knew that I would have to wind down the experiment. And when she died, I knew it must end. And then—my heart attack, preventing me from acting even on that suggestion until now.

"I apologize. The little charade with the blank tape and the singing—*I tricked you*. You had told me you had heard singing before. And I pretended that you had sent me a tape. I pretended I had talked to you from the Town Hall. But I had not.

"I am going to Town Hall today, and will call you up, and then bring this over to you so you can read it in black and white and see that I am right. You will have to admit now that witchcraft is a very tricky thing. You will have to admit that even the most discerning and non-believing can be forced to believe in what he does not want to believe—if others do!

Yours in psychology,
Ben Magruder."

I read the last paragraph and looked up at Don.

He was still grinning.

I stood up, throwing the letter down on the couch. "I'm going to fix something to eat," I said in an unsteady voice.

Poor Ben, I thought as I went out into the kitchen. He had been right. He had taught me a lesson. Only to die accidentally in a most gruesome manner.

Poor Ben.

I could weep for him—now that the fear had left me.

We ate and went to bed.

There was nothing to hold us apart now.

It was a dream, and a vivid one. Ben Magruder was in the darkness, and he was screaming: "No! No! Don't believe it, Aimee! *It's the devil's work!*"

And there was smoke and flame.

I smelled smoke.

I awoke suddenly, and sat upright in bed. I was perspiring freely. And I could smell the slight odor of smoke—a dead, rancid odor—but smoke.

It was very quiet in the bedroom. I could hear Don's

regular breathing. There was no light anywhere, and no movement other than the rising and falling of Don's chest.

A lie, Ben had said in the dream.

What was a lie?

The letter! Immediately, I began thinking what it had said, and I realized that if the letter was a lie, then the *other* things Ben had told me were true. That letter had turned everything upside down. What was true now?

I could almost see the neatly typed note in front of me, and hear Ben's voice as he had dictated the—

Then it came to me.

Ben Magruder *did not know how to type.* He always dictated what he did not write in his flowing, wild longhand.

Why had he had this letter typed? Perhaps he had not! Perhaps this letter was a lie!

I rose quietly and walked into the living room, still sniffing at the strange odor of dead smoke.

The letter lay on the couch where I had left it. I snapped on the floor lamp and stared at the typing. Now I realized that I should have noticed the difference right at the beginning.

A typewritten letter . . .

I held the paper closer. It was a familiar typewriter face. I thought it resembled our own portable that Don kept for his work away from the office. Where was that machine?

I went into the little study and pulled it out. I opened it up and studied it. Yes. It was the same kind of type as in the letter.

I rolled a sheet of paper into the machine and typed a few lines. Then I compared the letters with the letter Ben had written.

Now it was becoming positively frightening. The letters were identical—not similar. *Identical!* The same broken "f." The same widened "n." The same flat-topped "o."

The letter had been typed on our typewriter!

I could feel the cold air circulating around me, making me shake in my thin nightgown.

The same typewriter!

Cold, clammy perspiration crawled out on the surface of my skin. I could smell dead smoke.

I saw the shape on the desk before I realized what it was. I had been sitting there for some time, bemused, and I knew then that it was something that had been there before, but which I had never really looked at closely.

It was a corn cob pipe.

I reached out to pick it up, and then arrested my hand.

Don did not smoke! Nor did I!

How had that corn cob pipe gotten onto the desk Don used at night?

Or had it been there all the time, and I had simply not noticed it?

I reached out to touch it.

It was still warm.

I recoiled from the object and half stood, the blood pumping through me.

Where had I read recently about a pipe?

In the Salem book!

I moved quickly out into the living room, got the book, and went back into the study. Under the small desk lamp I leafed through the pages. Yes. One of the Salem witches had been a pipe-smoker. Not a man—but a woman. Sarah Good. Goody Good. Goodwife Good.

A pipe-smoker.

But what was this pipe doing in *my* house—

Something clicked in my mind. Witches. Wizards. Was not a male witch called a wizard? Yes. In Salem days. A wizard. And were not several of the Salem witches men? Yes. John Proctor. George Burroughs.

Could not a witch now—the one who was trying to kill me—be a man?

I shuddered. Yes!

Now, if Ben Magruder had identified the witch, and had been killed because of the identification, might not he have written the truth on paper before being run over by the hit-and-run car? And might not his letter have named names? And might not the *real witch* have found the letter and carefully re-written it to make out that there was no vengeance plot at all? That there was no witch trying to kill?

Yes!

And who—

I stood up quickly, snapped off the lamp, and moved back into the bedroom.

I stood there looking down at my husband's form.

And I could smell that stale smell of smoke again. I leaned over him and could smell it even more.

Stale smoke.

He stirred in his sleep and muttered something.

I leaned closer.

Latin?

I smelled sulphur.

Then Don stirred in his sleep and—*barked like a dog*!

I ran out of the room.

My only sanctuary was that tiny office at the Hall. I opened the door with my key and slipped inside. There was a small lamp near the desk and I turned it on. I was frightened and exhausted by the ordeal of the day and its grisly climax at my home!

There was no question in my mind now. Don was the guilty party, not Mrs. Venefica, or Ben Magruder, or Aimee Parris. Don Hammond!

I realized the truth of Ben Magruder's old statement now. Once you began thinking people were witches, there was no stopping! But of course, witch hunting had to stop somewhere. Someone was the real witch, and all the rest were not.

How had I been so blind?

Don had found me and married me, knowing my name was Parris. Possibly he had searched me out. He would now have his vengeance. I wondered who else he had killed in his days on earth in that body.

How many?

A Lewis? A Putnam? A Williams? Many others?

And he had done it all so cleverly. He had used the very background of the Hall where I worked to confuse me! I realized that it had been Don who had wanted to move to Coldwater, who had taken me along looking at houses. He must have known about the Hall, with Mrs. Venefica, and the cover for his witchcraft activities that existed there. He had found Lora Blake and had driven her mad!

He had used Mrs. Venefica to help him, of course. She was his *familiar*.

And he had used me. Those lapses of memory. Don was in my mind, directing me in my activities. Yes, I would have pushed Lora out the window if she had not jumped. I—with Don's will . . .

I was sick with anxiety and exhaustion.

I could feel a headache coming on.

My drawer was empty of aspirin. I had kept a box in there, but it was gone now. I could always awaken one of the girls.

No. I decided against that.

I knew Mrs. Grant had aspirin in her desk too. I had a key to the adjoining door—our two offices had a common wall between them. I went through into her office.

The light was dim, but I could see to open the desk drawer. It slid open easily. I glanced in the drawer. Mrs. Grant's calling cards. A white lace handkerchief with her initials on it. And the aspirins. I reached for the box in the right-hand corner. I had lifted it out and was about to shut the drawer once again when I saw the other blue handkerchief.

It resembled a light blue handkerchief that I myself used.

Then I saw the embroidery. A.L.P. Aimee Lorne Parris.

It was my hanky!

I stared a moment at it, and then I noticed that it was attached to something else, a rather lumpish shape.

Puzzled, I reached in and drew out the blue cloth wrapping and stared at it in consternation.

It was a poppet.

It wore my handkerchief for a dress. It had my face drawn in—blue eyes, red lips, light blond hair. It had a lock of my own hair! Across the chest was the name: AIMEE. It was so definitely *me* that I recoiled in horror.

There was a hole torn out of the head.

I felt sick.

I sank back into the chair and held the little horror in front of me. The hole in the head meant one thing: it was the hole through which my brain and mind and soul would be drawn so the witch could inhabit my body!

The poppet lay in my hands, inert and cold.

I was frightened to death.

Then I looked up.

The shadows were indistinct, but I could see her just inside the door, where she had appeared at that moment.

By magic?

Who knew?

She wore a red paragon bodice and very bright elbow-length gloves. She had her hair up in a fall, looking quite unlike the stern image of herself she allowed us to see at the Hall. I could see that she had on black stockings and a very tight-fitting, short skirt. Not at all like the gray dress she habitually wore.

She did not resemble the Mrs. Grant I knew.

"'Bridget Bishop,'" I said, for I remembered what I had read about the "red paragon bodice."

She smiled. "Yes, Betty."

"Aimee," I said.

"Betty," she corrected me. "Betty Parris."

"You're—you're crazy."

"No," she said. "But I've driven *you* there."

"Not really."

"Enough." She came around to the side of the desk. I clutched the poppet tighter to my chest. "You're a beautiful girl," she said in high glee. "It'll be like old times. Depart, Betty! Depart the body!"

She reached out to touch me and I felt fire sear my skin.

Chapter Seventeen

I pulled back from her touch and she smiled whimsically at my reaction. I needed time. I needed minutes, really. I remembered what Ben Magruder had written and I knew what to do, but it took time. I had to use up time.

Talk!

Talk, Aimee!

"It was you, all along," I said.

She smiled.

"You typed that false letter from Ben Magruder, and you used our typewriter to make me think it might be Don!"

"A simple trick," she said diffidently.

"And the pipe," I said. "You put it there when you got in the house and used the typewriter!"

"Yes. I had read Ben's papers, and I knew you would remember Sarah Good's pipe." She giggled. "Dear old Sarah! Dear old Goody Good! Too bad she went so quickly. She was a simple fool, really. It *was* her pipe, you know!" Mrs. Grant cackled in glee.

Or perhaps I should call her Bridget Bishop.

"But Don barked like a dog when I touched him tonight."

She chuckled mischievously. "In your half-demented state, my dear, you could imagine almost anything! Even the smell of smoke, you know."

"And it was you who forced me to grab up that knife and go after my husband."

"All part of the spell I cast on you, my lovely!"

"Why did you feel you had to rewrite Ben's letter?"

"He knew who I was," she said conspiratorially. "I couldn't allow him to tell you, could I? I mean, to warn you?"

"Perhaps not. And you—you killed Ben."

"Easily," she said softly. "My car. A moment's drive around the block, a few spells on the passersby so they would not remember to look at the car, and I had him." Her eyes narrowed in reminiscence. "Not like the old days when you could run a man through with a bodkin."

"Then you substituted the false letter and had it mailed to my house," I went on.

"If I had given it to you, you might have suspected something. What, I don't *really* know. You haven't been very alert."

I shook my head. "No. I admit that. And the nightmare? The dream about burning?"

"The very first move, my dear," she laughed. "The first day you came in to be interviewed I saw your name and I knew you would be on my list. And I simply used a little suggestion. It's called hypnotism now, post-hypnotic suggestion. But we who work with the Dark Man have always used it."

"And Lora Blake. You made her jump out the window."

"Yes. She was very easy to manipulate. She was just not all there, you know. And—uh—Mrs. Venefica softened her up for me."

"She was your 'familiar', wasn't she?" I asked, trying successfully to remember the term Ben had told me. "Mrs. Venefica."

"Yes. More than my familiar, actually," Bridget Bishop went on. "She worked with me, and for Him."

"And Willa Gayle—you killed her, too."

"Yes. Before my familiar moved in here, you know. That was all on my own."

"The garroting?"

"A scottish custom I have always been very much opposed to, as has the Dark Power. It seemed fitting to

178

destroy her in this manner. A bit of getting back at the law, you know."

"And Ellen Putnam."

"Putnam!" snapped Bridget Bishop. "A pox on the Putnams! She was easy! I simply cast one tiny spell on her, made a poppet, and she was done! *Done!* I put the poppet in a pan of water—"

"Please," I said, turning away from her. I still held the poppet of myself behind my back, and was working with it frantically. "Don't let's talk about it."

"That awful man guessed, of course," Bridget mused. "That Ben Magruder. He was most intelligent. He found the key to the plot. He saw that the names were repeated. He knew that Willa Gayle was Abigail Williams. And he knew that Ellen Putnam was Ann Putnam."

"And that *I* was Elizabeth Parris!"

"Yes, my dear!" she cried out in glee. "And you were Elizabeth Parris!"

"And why do you intend to kill me, Mrs. Grant?"

"For that lovely body," she said with a wild laugh. Her eyes seemed to burn with fire. She reached out again, and seized me by the shoulder. I could feel the chill of her grip and the fire inside me as she touched my flesh.

I shook with ague.

"Out, Betty! Out, Betty Parris! Empty thy body so Bridget, thy Mistress, can enter!"

I had the poppet fixed now. I could feel it behind me. I had removed my blue handkerchief from the poppet's body; I had torn the hair off; I had slipped one of Mrs. Grant's calling cards into the inside of the poppet's body; I had stretched the body, elongating it to conform to Mrs. Grant's physical characteristics.

I said, "I won't go, Bridget!"

"Who calls me Bridget!" cried the woman, her eyes mad with dark fire. "Who *dares* call me Bridget?"

"I do," I said quietly.

"Only the Master of Darkness can address me thus! Master, appear! Master, aid me!"

I stood and twisted the poppet behind me, turning so

she could not see it but would be attracted by the movement.

Her eyes flicked downward, and a flash of understanding crossed her face.

"*You* have it! Give it to me, Betty! Give me the poppet!"

"No!" I screamed, and began to move from her.

She grabbed me and spun me around.

I fought her off, holding the doll away from her. She turned, saw the letter opener on the desk, and grasped it in her right hand. I twisted from her and ran around the desk.

She reached out with the letter opener and slashed through the air at me.

"Vanish, Betty! Leave thy body!"

I shook my head.

"Give me the doll!" cried Bridget Bishop.

I held it out to her.

She took one look at it and sent the letter opener slashing through the middle of its cloth body. I let the poppet go and dropped it to the desk top.

The letter opener fell to the floor.

Bridget Bishop stood still and in shock, behind the desk. She stared wide-eyed at the torn, slashed poppet.

It had a long rip through the middle. It did not wear the blue handkerchief that had belonged to me. It now wore the handkerchief I had seen in the desk drawer beside the aspirins. The handkerchief had Mrs. Grant's initials on it.

And the face had changed, although I had not tried to change it at all.

Now it resembled Mrs. Grant.

The head was torn.

I stood, rooted to the spot, and watched Mrs. Grant. Bridget Bishop.

One moment she was standing there in an attitude of arrested frenzy, and in the next she was slowly folding in on herself, and falling to the floor.

And then she was lying there quite still and lifeless.

I leaned over her.

She was not dressed in the red paragon bodice or the

long black stockings at all. I had simply imagined it. Or she had forced me to see her that way. She was dressed quite simply in the plain gray dress she usually wore around the Hall. And there was a strange lifelessness in her expression. No smile. No gleam in the eye. No half-mad zest. She looked exactly like the plain, drab, unglamorous Mrs. Grant always looked.

I touched her wrist.
No pulse.
I checked her breathing.
No breath.
She was dead.

"It sometimes happens that way," said Dr. Kingsley an hour later. "I don't know if you were aware of it, or not, young lady, but Mrs. Grant was dying of a malignant carcinoma. For some reason her entire body just seemed to give out all at once tonight. These things happen in medicine; there is often no explanation for it." His eyes narrowed. "There is something of hopelessness, a sense of defeat, that prevents the human body from fighting off death. And so—" He shrugged.

"Yes," I said in a soft voice.

"It's such a shame the two of them should go within a day of one another," he mused. "They were such staunch companions."

"Oh?" I said, puzzled.

"Yes. Mrs. Grant has been here for some time at the Hall. She sent for Mrs. Venefica a year and a half ago to help her out."

"I didn't know they were that good friends," I said.

"Yes. They grew up together, and were always very thick."

"Did you know them?"

"Oh, yes. I treated them both. They roomed together for years at the old Carter Nelson Hotel."

"I didn't know that."

"That was before Mrs. Venefica married. Actually, Venefica was her second husband. Chap by the name of Bill Welch was her first."

I blinked my eyes. "Welch was her previous name?"

"Oh, yes."

"Do you know her maiden name?"

"I certainly do. She was my teacher in Grammar School. Miss Good. It was quite a joke with us. That was her name. Miss Sarah Good."

Chapter Eighteen

The excitement from the incident at Fairfield Residence Hall continued for some weeks. The news media ate up the story.

"Salem Witches Visit Connecticut Town," the headlines in the papers read.

Tom Denver led the pack. He had always been interested in the garroting case of Willa Gayle. And now that the story was once again back in the news—and in such a sensational context—he dropped everything else and camped out in Coldwater covering every angle of the story.

Research by such a pack of dedicated journalists dug out some interesting facts. Not only had Willa Gayle (Abigail Williams), Ellen Putnam (Ann Putnam), and Lora Blake (Mary Warren) been killed, but a girl named Jane Hubbard had also met her death in a strange "accident" in her room on the fourth floor of the Hall five years ago. That would be the accuser Elizabeth Hubbard of Salem, if you followed the parallels that Ben Magruder had laboriously constructed.

The media stuck to the story and squeezed it dry of everything it had, and then suddenly, one day, they were all gone and Coldwater slowly began returning to normal.

The Board of Directors of Fairfield Residence Hall met and then called me in to discuss the possibility of my taking over as Mrs. Grant's successor. I demurred and told them I had to discuss this with my husband, which I did. In the sudden euphoria attendant to the winding up of the strange nightmares I had been having, Don decided to give me his permission and I told the Board that I would be glad to sign a contract for three years.

And I did.

It was still an incredible story, no matter how you looked at it. I spent many hours with Don trying to figure out how it had happened, and trying to fathom the strange quirks and twists of the human mind.

I continued my analysis with Dr. Strachey, but there were not too many more strange byways of my own mental processes to examine. We came through after several months with a fairly logical assessment of my own psychotic situation. I had no deep-seated problem at all, but simply an inner conflict that had resulted from too strict repression in my adolescence.

Dr. Strachey tried to break down my inhibitions in regard to sex and physical attraction, and I think I am well on my way to being a better human being for it.

Don says I am more relaxed now—but he never had any real complaints anyway. So much for *that*.

Several weeks after the last of the excitement had died down, we invited Dr. Strachey to our house for dinner, and after we had eaten, we went out onto the back porch and sat there in the dark listening to the night sounds and discussing the strange ramifications of Coldwater's invasion by the daemons.

In Mrs. Grant's papers was found the original letter that Ben Magruder had written and intended to give me the day he was killed in front of Town Hall. I brought out the letter to read it to Dr. Strachey. Remember, this was Ben's final disposition of the case of Bridget Bishop, painstakingly put together just before he had been run over by the hit-and-run driver.

"Dear Aimee," the letter began in Ben's sprawling hand.

"Your life is in extreme danger, for you are on the death list of a woman who practices witchcraft, who, in fact, *is* a witch.

"Her name is Bridget Bishop, and she was hanged for witchcraft in 1692 on Salem Hill, but she has returned to the living to wreak vengeance on those who cried out against her and sentenced her to death.

"You are on the list to be killed because your maiden name was Parris, and because you came from Salem. Although it cannot be proven that you are a direct descendent of Elizabeth Parris—it would hardly be likely that you are because the name Parris disappeared with Elizabeth's marriage almost three hundred years ago—Bridget Bishop is convinced that by killing you she will wreak vengeance on yet another liar of the group who put her to death on the gallows.

"Three girls from the Hall have been murdered already in Coldwater: Willa Gayle, garroted and poisoned; Ellen Putnam, a suicide under strange circumstances; and Lora Blake, who jumped out of a window and died.

"Bridget Bishop believes that Willa Gayle is Abigail Williams come to earth once again, and Abigail Williams is on her list of 1692 accusers. Ellen Putnam is Ann Putnam come to earth again, and Ann Putnam is on Bridget's list. So is Lora Blake, whose mother's name was Warren, and who represents Mary Warren, another accuser. And you represent Elizabeth Parris, the famous Betty Parris, daughter of Samuel Parris the minister of Salem.

"I assure you that you are next on Bridget Bishop's list. And she has killed before. To kill Willa Gayle, Ellen Putnam, and Lora Blake, Bridget Bishop instigated a witch coven at Fairfield Residence Hall and brought the girls into her 'circle of magic.'

"I do not have proof, but I assume that Bridget put curses on these girls by making poppets of them, labeling them neatly, and treating the poppets as she wanted the girls treated.

"I believe she tied a wire around the neck of Willa Gayle's likeness, and twisted it until Willa was dead.

"I believe she submerged the likeness of Ellen Putnam in a saucepan of water, until Ellen was drowned.

"I believe she dropped the likeness of Lora Blake from a height until she too was dead.

"And I believe she is in some fashion causing a likeness of you to go through tortures of the damned until you are likewise dead, in what fashion I do not truly know.

"Bridget Bishop is not alone in this enterprise. She is supported by a practicing witch whose real name I do not know, but whom I suspect to be another one of the original Salem witches hanged.

"Together these two have listed the names of those they will kill for vengeance on their hanging in 1692.

"You know Bridget Bishop as Mrs. Grant. I suspect Mrs. Venefica, or Sarah Welch, of being another in the list, Sarah Good, perhaps, but I cannot prove it.

"Find the poppet they have made of you. Remove all identifying marks from it that resemble you. And leave the Hall forever.

"Please do not make light of this letter. I will be with you when you read it and answer any questions you have. Know that I do have proof!

"I suspect, actually, that Bridget Bishop may not be trying to destroy you, but to force your mind and spirit out of your body and steal your body so she can live on in your flesh. If you do not take stern counter-measures and practice effective counter-spells, you—your soul—will be forced into limbo for eternity.

"Have mercy on an old man's anxiety, and leave the Hall before this scarlet diabolist controls you!

Ben."

When I had finished reading the letter out loud, Dr. Strachey leaned back in his chair and sighed.

"Hysterical utterance," he said sadly. "Too bad. Ben Magruder was a serious man, involved in serious research. But he had it all wrong. It can be explained quite scientifically, without all that mumbo-jumbo of his."

"How?" Don asked skeptically. I could have kissed

him. He wanted Ben to be right. So did I. Poor old Ben.

Dr. Strachey cleared his throat.

"The woman was born Bridget Bishop," he said. We knew this now because the papers had been full of it. "I do not believe any more than you do that she was really a reincarnation of the original Bridget Bishop who was hanged on Gallows Hill in Salem Town. It is tempting to see such a dramatic reincarnation as the truth.

"But it is more likely that her early life was simply an unhappy one. Born of poor parents, she was brought up by an aunt and an uncle who had no use for her mother and father, nor for her, really. And they put up with her rather than take her into their hearts.

"Because she felt rejected, she took to reading books for friends and companions. The foster parents lived in a remote country section of Connecticut, and Bridget had no friends to speak of. Because the aunt and uncle were unfriendly and unattractive people, no school friends would come to visit her.

"She grew more and more into a recluse whose only recreation was reading. She devoured books and finally, one day, she found a book on the Salem trials. And that was when she discovered a fantastic thing. A Bridget Bishop was one of the burned witches. A scarlet woman. Owner of two taverns! *She* was Bridget Bishop. That was her name, was it not? Could she not possibly be the reincarnation of Bridget Bishop?

"The obsession took hold of her. She went to college and there met Sarah Good, from another small town in Connecticut—Coldwater. Another witch from Salem! And so from this coincidence, her belief in her identity as a witch grew. Bridget and Sarah both took up the study of diabolism and demonology, and became practicing witches.

"Their friendship strengthened through the years. Their experiments with diabolism continued, although on a subdued scale as they were each married.

"Bridget's husband died some years later, and she got a job at the Fairfield Residence Hall. Here, with making of poppets by the time she made yours, Aimee."

I nodded. "Indeed she had!"

"I'll go along with Ben Magruder on that point. I think she did indeed torment Jane Hubbard's poppet, and somehow strangled it or caused it to be unable to breathe. Whatever, Jane smothered in her bed. The death was judged a death by accident, and Bridget was not questioned.

"Ben Magruder admitted once that if someone believed in witchcraft, it *did* exist. This is quite possible. I do not for one instant think that Jane Hubbard smothered because Bridget Bishop tormented her likeness in the form of a poppet. But we must remember that Jane Hubbard had at first joined the witch's coven and had signed the pact with the Devil, so-called, to do so. In her mind the very fact that she had turned against God and walked with the Devil meant she was in danger. With Bridget Bishop muttering incantations against her, and possibly cursing her to her face and telling her she would die, Jane did, indeed, become sick.

"Perhaps Bridget strangled her in bed, or held the pillow over her face to suffocate her. Whatever it was, Jane Hubbard died of suffocation in bed. Do you see what I'm getting at?"

I spoke up. "Yes. You mean that Jane was psychotic to a degree, after having become a Devil-worshipper, and therefore susceptible to self-destruction."

"Yes," said Dr. Strachey.

"Go on," said Don.

"But then another torment came—a *second* girl who would not cooperate with her and threatened to reveal her actions to the Board. Willa Gayle. But now Bridget knew how to analyze these demons sent to torment her, and she reasoned that Willa Gayle was actually Abigail Williams by a twisted anagram. And so she constructed another poppet in the shape and features of Willa. And she tormented it and tied a strong wire around the throat of the doll. I think, quite probably, Bridget gar- he girl and carried her out into the woods herself. Anyway, that was the end of the second tormentor sent by her enemies from out of the past.

"Then came Ellen Putnam, and Bridget knew she was Ann Putnam, and she fashioned another poppet and went to work again. This poppet she threw into a pan of water. Eventually, Ellen Putnam drowned herself. I would suggest that many of the problems the Putnam girl and the Gayle girl suffered might easily have been induced into their mind by suggestion, or hypnotism, along with the judicious use of certain drugs. There *were* traces of drugs found in the stomach of Willa Gayle, you recall.

"I do not doubt that Bridget Bishop did make poppets. Her technique of tormenting the dolls simply induced in her mind the torments she would use in person. Then, when the victims were half-unconscious from the influence of drugs, ingested through tea or coffee, she would hypnotize them into taking whatever action she wanted them to."

Dr. Strachey sighed. "After Ellen Putnam's death, there were a few months of relative calm, and then Bridget's old friend Sarah Good suddenly appeared. Her husband had died, and she had no money. So Bridget hired Sarah, who was now known as Mrs. Venefica—Mrs. Witch, in Latin—and the two of them settled down at the Hall into an orgy of demonology.

"Now Bridget could relax. The onus of the work was on Sarah and Sarah loved to sound the incantations and sing the songs. So Bridget sat by and watched for more signs.

"And Lora Blake came. Bridget had become quite adept now at poppetry and spell-casting, and she arranged for Lora to jump out the window. We know, of course, that Lora was disturbed and simply the victim of an advanced suicidal complex.

"But before Lora Blake came, Bridget had hired you, Aimee. And you were special. Elizabeth Parris, Betty Parris, was the daughter of Samuel Parris, the man most responsible for the hanging of Bridget Bishop. He had *started* the witch hunt.

"She was planning something *perfectly horr-*

189

for you. She destroyed Abigail Williams, Ann Putnam, Mary Warren, and Elizabeth Hubbard, but she would *use* you. For, about this time, she had been told by Dr. Kingsley that she had inoperable cancer and must die soon.

"But she was a witch! She could not die! By this time, she firmly believed that she was the Bridget Bishop of 1692. And she conceived the idea that she could live on in your body. I believe Ben Magruder was right about that. Bridget began systematically to force you to empty your mind for hours at a time, so that there was simply a blank in your memory—and in your *aliveness*, let's say. Bridget had only to *concentrate* herself into your body, emptied of your psyche, and she would make the transition she sought. I am convinced that this is what she dreamed of doing."

Dr. Strachey looked at me. "Because you were involved in a mental conflict of your own, which you hardly knew about until you visited me, you thought you were being possessed. And so you were. Bridget used post-hypnotic suggestion, as she explained in her false letter, supposedly written by Ben Magruder.

"To her horror Bridget found that Ben Magruder had discovered the pentacle under the doormat—put there, more or less as a lark, by the coven—and the herbs growing in Sarah Good's room. And he suspected someone was trying to possess you, Aimee.

"Bridget watched Ben Magruder and found out that he had done a great deal of research. Then Ben Magruder penetrated her identity, found that *she* was the one behind the spells and the deaths. He started out with his notes and the explanation he had written to you in longhand, and crossed the street. Bridget killed him.

"Then she decided she would have to use your house, Aimee, to transplant her soul into your body. She made you stage that knife scene with your husband, then forced you to write a note that you were going to your mother's. She delivered the false letter of Ben's to your husband after writing it out on your typewriter and leaving Sarah's old corn cob pipe in the study.

"Then all she had to do was wait for you to run out of the house and come to the Hall. She simply didn't figure that you could outwit her at her own game. Changing the identity of the poppet, as you did, was a master stroke. It demolished her own psychological self-confidence, and caused her fears of mortality—she knew she was dying—to overwhelm her. The shock of the sudden withdrawal of her ability to perform magic very simply destroyed her. Her own resistance to the pain of her illness diminished, and the suffering became too much to bear, and her physical body ceased to exist."

We sat there a moment in silence.

Dr. Strachey cleared his throat carefully. "There's a fallacy in all this 'direct lineal descendent' theory, of course, that is rather obvious. A woman loses her family name at her marriage. The second generation may carry the name as a middle name, but after that it is gone. Think how many generations passed from the first Bridget Bishop to the present one!" He shook his head. "No. It simply could not be she. I'm happy I am able to understand the whole thing in sensible scientific terms."

"You're so right, Dr. Strachey," I said, and sank back in my chair with Ben Magruder's paper in my hands.

Don smiled at me.

At least the nasty business of Bridget Bishop and Sarah Good was over. I wondered who the next one to try would be. Sarah Wild? Susanna Martin? Alice Parker?

No matter. She will be easy to identify this time. You learn a little something going through a strange hunt like this one.

Right, Bridget? Sarah?

AVON ◆ GOTHIC ORIGINALS
MASTERPIECES OF SUSPENSE!

Crucible of Evil — Lyda Belknap Long

Amanda Lescot left her childhood home, Lescot Manor Hall, to escape an evil too horrible to be borne. But in a sudden flash of mysterious and terrifying circumstances, her sinister ordeal began again—leading to a fearsome struggle to overcome dark and mysterious forces!

(19646—95¢)

The Spirit of Brynmaster Oaks — Anne J. Griffin

A beautiful young bride learns of her husband's sinister past—and the terrifying vision that will come to haunt them both—as they are plunged into a strange web of suffocating evil!

(19737—95¢)

Stark Island — Lynna Cooper

Inez came to Stark House to catalogue the library, but one night as she took a moonlight swim in Deepdene Pool, she saw a pair of bright eyes watching her from the shrubbery. Thus began her encounter with a horrible creature, and a macabre figure in the family mausoleum!

(19463—95¢)

Where better paperbacks are sold, or directly from the publisher. Include 25¢ per copy for mailing; allow three weeks for delivery.

Avon Books, Mail Order Dept., 250 West 55th Street, New York, N. Y. 10019